TAURUS

ALSO BY JOSEPH SMITH

The Wolf

TAURUS

JOSEPH SMITH

JONATHAN CAPE
LONDON

Published by Jonathan Cape 2010

2 4 6 8 10 9 7 5 3 1

Illustrations by John Spencer

First published in Great Britain in 2010 by
Jonathan Cape
Random House, 20 Vauxhall Bridge Road,
London SW1V 2SA

www.rbooks.co.uk

Addresses for companies within The Random House Group Limited can be found at:
www.randomhouse.co.uk/offices.htm

The Random House Group Limited Reg. No. 954009

A CIP catalogue record for this book
is available from the British Library
ISBN 9780224089975

The Random House Group Limited supports The Forest Stewardship Council (FSC),
the leading international forest certification organisation. All our titles that are printed
on Greenpeace approved FSC certified paper carry the FSC logo. Our paper
procurement policy can be found at www.rbooks.co.uk/environment

Typeset by Palimpsest Book Production Limited, Grangemouth, Stirlingshire

Printed and bound in Germany by GGP Media GmbH, Pößneck

CHAPTER I

The sun is beating into the darkness of my back.

I feel its heat pushing down on me, trying to force me towards the hotter ground of dust and stone. The earth is dead and cracked, a lifeless thing on which cling blunted stems of green, and there are ants and others that always seem to be active just beneath its surface. But the earth's opposite, sky, now open and unscratched, is different – it feels to me that it is alive and is able to look down with the eyes I give it of sun and moon. Often clouds form that can turn and disappear, and then reds and oranges that suddenly streak upward from the horizon. I have watched these things as they change into the stars and make new shapes like clouds – not as clear and strong as in the day, but because they are there every night and are always the same I learn them and follow them as they twist around sickeningly, a whole night feeling no longer than a sunset. The stars and their forms fade at the end of night but I keep them, not only the images I have in my head but also perhaps the drops that form on the stones. The mists that sometimes hang in strange smears and that I walk through and inhale might be these same things too, after falling.

But this heat that I stand beneath now makes those cool mornings, when the ground is slippery and the air dampens my flanks, seem like fantasy. It makes the things I want to believe seem unreal in the absence of what is felt. In the middle of the day, to turn and walk a few steps is to be drained of everything except an awareness of the sun, how it takes everything out of the still air and bakes almost all the life out of the ground. It is like a weight – more than the weight of all the flesh I carry – and while muscle can be felt lifted and falling with my movements, in the heat there is no movement and for a short time it feels unending, so that I think that I am to the sky what a stone is beneath my hoof – not crushed but pinned, solidified.

My neck loosens and I look down at the ground. It has veins running over it and stones and rare greenery twisting upward, up towards the thing above that is doing all this, and I think that if I were a plant I would grow downward, I would grow away from the sun and the absent step that can crush a year's growth. The earth around me has a border, a fence running in a line visible and invisible, its posts clear but the mesh in between just a shimmer in both sun and mist. I am enclosed, protected, so that I know every step in this paddock, all the tiny empty channels in the earth from when they appear in late spring; and I see all the plants that grow here, learning what progress is for them. I have this ground beneath me and most nights the forms above so that sometimes I feel that I'm not heavy with the flesh around my withers but am suspended, hanging unafraid between the things I attend to.

There is a crack in the ground that is running from under me towards one of the posts a few steps away, as if by the pounding in of the post and the stamping of my leg we have formed it together. If I follow the line from me to beyond the post it leads slightly uphill to the house, a huge white slab blazing out of the otherwise dull brown and occasional green surrounds, yet in front of it is an even greater shock – bright green grass surrounded by flowers of all different colours, as if the house was casting not a shadow down the hill but its opposite. I raise my head into the heat to stare at this and allow myself to think that it is the life of the sky that is striking down on the house and bursting from its side with colour. But I feel nothing as I think this.

And I feel nothing but the heat and my own weight as I turn away from the house and its gardens and look downhill, at the dry, rough land rolling downward and then back up a little before becoming horizon. It is the same in each direction – the same prospect of dust and scattered plant growth, the same absence of anything larger than something I could step on except the scarce trees, standing alone and distanced from each other. The only change is if I turn and look uphill again but away from the house, where there is the barn that I share and attached to it the low fence made of the same wood that the barn is, and which from where I see it now curves out towards me like a stomach.

I look at this curve and imagine the feel of my horn pressed against it, scoured along its side, its tip running over the gaps in the wood to make a noise like the one we hear before the boy appears in the brightness of the barn doorway, a stick in his hand. How soft and old is that wood? Perhaps if I were able to stand before it, lower my head and pitch my weight forward, it would lean slightly like the posts of the paddock fence do. I take a few steps and a little dust rises from under me, the earth making quiet noises beneath the weight that pushes at it. Even if I scrape and stamp at the earth it is quiet! All is quiet at this time of day, as if I have been abandoned. I am left standing alone, looking aimlessly and listlessly in one direction and another, the only movement the muscles of my neck and withers as I turn my head – or the infrequent throwing forward of a hoof.

I walk to the part of the paddock that is nearest the house, the blaze of white and sudden colour a tired but reliable fascination. I search for movement, shifting my head slightly behind the fence, looking through the bright metal that disappears but can obscure the object beyond. There is no sign of them – no sign of the dogs either – not even the plants or flowers move in the breeze because the only breeze there is is the swaying of my head slightly behind the fence, watching as the little threads of silver add themselves as another growth, another strangeness where there should be scrub and rock. And mostly I am content to do this – I am satisfied to stare like this and then turn and push my weight through the dust and air until I reach the other side of the paddock.

But sometimes, like now, my breaths don't go in as deep – I seem to be floundering for breath before I realise and snort out so as to breathe in deeply, kicking at the ground as if it were the thing trying to block the air from my insides. Suddenly I feel as if there is something in the paddock with me, something so real that I turn to meet it with dull annoyance pricking at my back. I turn and face the heat of the shimmering air and though I am afraid I hope that there is something there – an enemy of flesh that threatens what I must protect, a thing that I can lower my head before and ram into and feel its mass jolting down my spine. But again there is nothing and by the time I have turned and looked for my enemy, staring through the emptiness of land to where it meets the blue of the sky, the desire I had is forgotten; it has escaped as if as trifling as the will to swish my tail.

I let it escape and feel the sun move over me, its heat sloping around the curve of my shoulders to weigh on the base of my neck. Now there is something behind me – a sound – the sound of footsteps light and steady on the dust and I turn my head to see the boy coming towards the paddock from the house, pushing the barrow in front of him. I step quickly so that I face this movement, raising my head as he approaches, keen to see if the barrow he pushes is full or empty and know whether the course of this day will end here in the paddock or back in the barn. I notice him as well, the boy, while I strain my head upward, smelling the air for the feed. He is hidden while his hands are on the barrow, becoming something fused and ugly that makes him a smaller and weaker thing, but I can still see his manner as he pushes at the thing in front of him. It used to be that I could tell whether it was full of feed or not by the way he pushed it, but he has become large enough that it makes no difference any more and what is clearer from looking at him now is that he is calm – when he becomes separate from it he will make his movements without the burning anger that sometimes sees his long thin body twist quickly, hurling a stick into the scrub, beating at the earth or the fence with the metal of his spade, a mewling growl like a dog's coming from his throat.

Now he is nearer the fence than I am, and with him dropping the barrow it is as if they have been cleaved apart, the metal falling away dead to make a quiet scrape on the ground and the boy straightening, sloughing off the skin of his labour, and I see him clearly – the glistening black on his head, the long thin flow of limb and body covered in something the colour of the earth, the eyes a brown but more like a pair of setting suns than the thing he and I stand on. With a few slow footfalls I move closer to the fence, watching him, looking to see into the barrow that is empty and then turning to him again. He comes towards me, the springing youth in his step that used to be of no harm but to himself, is now in his grasp, a part of his spirit, a thing dangerous to those around him, and as he comes closer I feel a weak fear that does nothing to my heart or lungs except echo thinly through them. Even the other thing that his approach breeds – the urge that makes me scrape slightly at the ground and flick my ears and snort – this too is hollow, a reaction born of habit, a resonance of my own youth when fear was real and unwelcome, a choking thing as if the air had turned to dust.

And I am not afraid when he leaves the barrow and comes right up to the fence, his arms swinging at his sides, his head down and watching the rocky ground in front of him. And when he crouches down to twist at the pipe leading into the paddock – when he becomes a smaller thing again – I trot forward towards the mesh so that its holes are almost my nostrils, smelling him, looking at him as his whole body twists at the tap and then turns with the screeching metal. I look down at this boy and think that yes, if the fence were not there holding me in I would take him up on my back and feel his small body rolling down it to

smack onto the ground behind me. Then I would turn and have
him as the sun has me, as I have the stones beneath my hooves.
I can hear the water trickling into the trough away to my side
and though I am thirsty I don't turn away from him because I
cannot. I find as I watch him now making the metal squeak with
just a turn of his wrist that there is a disgust in me, like a sour
liquid rattling in the bottom of my lungs, a thing that is in my
blood and that can move my body more than my mind into
terrible nights – nights as long as years of unfeeling.

This figure before me can cause this? No. This hatred is for
the fence that stops me getting to him – the ugly, bent ring of
wood and metal that circles me and he can hide behind. Then
he stands quickly and my neck and ears follow his rising movement, his head and shoulders appearing above the fence in a
sudden clarity that lets me see every heavy strand of dark hair
coming almost over his shining eyes, the muscles of his jaw
rippling as he clenches his teeth together and the fine, brittle
dents of his nose. I breathe deeply to smell him, to try and
bring the distance between us to nothing. Would I really take
him on my horns if the fence was absent? Perhaps I would
just walk to him, pulled forward by his eyes, wanting only to
be closer to his lithe grace and the power that lashes within

him like a wind around a fire. There is a malice in him – it fills him as clearly as the fresh water that sits in my trough and I think I must be thirsty for both because it does not stop me from watching him, from enjoying his movements of thin flesh on even thinner bones, seeing how there are still traces of awkwardness from where his body has grown away from its youth.

His body tenses and I think that he will lift his foot and walk away, but as he turns to profile the dirt crunches softly and he stops, his eyes returning to mine. And quickly I know that his mind is on me as well because I can see myself – I can see the large black shape planted on short legs that he sees, the thick shoulders and neck and the huge broad head with its horns pointing skyward. I swish my tail and snort and stamp and I can see a bull, doing these things, standing behind a fence with rough brown earth and pale sky meeting at a line behind him where he stands. I feel my heart moving inside me and know that it moves in this bull, which is very close now because the boy is studying me, he is looking at the muscle that fills my shoulders and rump, the width of bone where hoof meets leg, the large head as hard as a stone with only the flesh-like wetness of eye and nostril as a weakness, a sudden reminder that I am not really made of rock, but one that is quickly forgotten by the tapering cruelty of the horns, long and twisted, apex of the beast.

The boy has had his fill of me – he is raising his head from the trough because now I can see myself only in glimpses, in shifting images that are clear for a moment and then disappear. I have to wring them from him – these insights of myself – I have to pull them out as I do the forms from the stars, standing in the night with my neck burning, struggling to keep my head upward to see more than just above the horizon. He has come right back up to the fence and I am startled when his hand shoots upward above one of the wooden posts, the fabric on his arm flapping and the hand pausing in the air before coming to rest. He leans on the post as I sometimes do but from the other side, towards me, and his weight is nothing to the wood or the earth it sits in. His body slightly slanted in the air, he looks at me – his mouth opens and I hear his voice, quiet and not thickened with rage but still with a bright edge of malice, a sharpness as he speaks to me – and I am confused because I see in him something that locks my eyes to him, that does not make me turn away.

Because often I hold him in my sight. His sharp eyes and

nose are like the little lizards that sometimes can be seen at the edge of the paddock or in the barn, flinging themselves at insects, missing, falling and then scurrying back up the wall after the same quarry. He is like these creatures, snatching at life as he used to snatch at his breath when he was younger, his face a mess of wetness. I admire the force that moved his arm to startle me but think too that it is unpleasant – in the same way that the lizard's eager jumping is ugly, futile, somehow repugnant. He stops speaking softly to me, but I can see in his movements that he is thinking about me again, or something like me. In the little flick of his fingers, in the flexing of the spine where it is attached by arm to the post and ground, and in the direction of his gaze and the eyes themselves – in all of these movements I read signs of myself, as clear as if I were looking down into a huge trough to see an outline of head and horns in the water. To look at him now is to feel an echo of what I am made of – not a thin reflection of sound but one strong enough to be confused with its origin – and I am gripped as I watch, as I see the things unfurl from him – the sunlight and shade, the colour of red wall and yellow earth, a man more like a bird than a man in bright colours and dancing in front of a bull, but far more of a beast than I – and suddenly the dance is over, the man is no longer moving and arcing with beauty but has become part of the red wall, is sitting slumped in the dirt against it. I look to the boy's eyes, wondering if he will turn away and end this vision, but he doesn't and I see what it is that makes him think this many times when he watches me, what it is that joins he and I in some way that nothing else does: it is the moment where the bull, quicker than a dog, as quick as a cat, skips forward as if without moving to catch the man on the end of his horns and lift him in the air, keeping him there by the movement that is now pushing them both forward before throwing him and turning away, the man continuing his flight to land against the wall and slump into the dirt.

I know that the blood that lifted that man is in me! I can hear it and feel it every time the boy has this memory – this memory that he loves and that excites him. But I feel nothing of his excitement and none of the pain that he does, the thing that grabs him in the belly and twists him into ecstasy. The blood is there – I must be joined to the very bull that the boy watches in his mind, throwing the man – yet I must have some-thing missing because all I can do is share a fascination for the movements and the feelings that formed them. I share the memory with the boy but not its furnace: a slumped form and upturned palms in yellow sand unlinked to the empty lust I have to run at the mirages in my paddock, the ones I imagine clawing at me when my back is turned.

I snort and turn quickly away from the boy, frightening him so that his arm comes away from the post. I lift my hooves and push my body through the air, feeling the shifting masses of flesh around me and beyond them the heat of the day, the dust, the weight of the sun. There is a fencepost that I am looking for and I head for it before realising I am mistaken and so turn slightly to the next – then I am standing next to it, seeing the small point of metal sticking out from the wood towards me. I edge forward and lower my head, angling it so that the horns do not touch too much wood or metal. I push against the post and feel it move slightly in the earth. Then, after a while, I feel the wonderful sharpness of the metal as the nail goes beyond hair and membrane into my blood, cooling it, sending ripples of pain and coldness as far as my shoulder and the bottom of my cheek. Shaded this way from the sky and its eye of the sun, I remain standing there for a long time, I alone breaking through the skin of heat that covers everything here and makes it all insensate.

When I raise my head the boy is looking at me and I know I must be bleeding a little from the new hole in my neck. He is saying something and I know it is the name he and the others call me; this makes me stop to listen to the deeply silent afternoon and the repetitive noise he makes to disturb it, even though it is just noise, and means nothing to me – nothing more than the bark of the dog.

CHAPTER 2

I am breathing lightly, my head lowered and looking upward through the large gaps in the wooden posts and bars that surround me – that make a shape without curve of the space of trodden earth and straw that I stand on. It is dark, but there are grey flecks appearing on the walls and above on the roof – little marks of light that will grow to long yellow bars scraping through the darkness, showing the motes and the thick angles of wood that divide us – that mean I can look only at the large grey shape opposite me with its long head hanging over the fence and its ears pointed back while lower, although obscured by the rough wood, I can see how one leg is bent, its hoof curled backward so that its sharp edge bites into the ground.

I continue to breathe softly, watching it breathe as well to take the thick and moist air of the barn into it silently as it sleeps. And again I must marvel at this creature – this horse that can stand and roll the air in and out of itself with hardly a flicker of movement as it does now. And then at other times with sweat foaming at its neck it can send to me a storm of movement and sound as it gallops from one end of its paddock to another, suddenly turning in deeply slanted circles, more a part of the air than something that must breathe it. It is a creature of change – a thing of changes – and that is why I stand here with my head lowered because I want to see it wake up. I want to see those large eyes open and the big head snap up – the bolt of life shoot through the legs and the slight stagger of consciousness as it realises where it is. I must witness these things and will stand like this every morning that I am in the barn, because to see them flow into the Grey as he wakes is like watching a leaf in violent wind, or an object separating from the boy's hand. It is to see something powerless before its surroundings and sensitive to forces other than itself, and this grips me – it is the thing *I* become powerless before, no longer ruled by the things that shimmer through me.

Now there is suddenly more light and it comes from the side and low down near the ground, a bright grey shape starting as a slit and growing into a large hole like an eye – but an eye that blinks with a scraping noise – and then bursting through it a pointed snout and ears, little white teeth and the whole aspect of it eager and distasteful – the small dog pushing itself through the hole on its stomach, tilting its head at one angle and then another as it does so, its tongue leaking out to the side over its teeth. Then it is through and the hole closes behind it, shutting out the brightness as the broken wood falls back into place. The dog stands and shakes itself in a quick, lusty little action and then it begins trotting about the space between the Grey and I, head down and stump of a tail up, poking and smelling everything, all with a horrible quickness and zeal that disgusts me – that makes me snort and press against the wood of the fence.

The dog does not turn or even move an ear in my direction and instead I look back to the Grey, peering up at him through the gap in the wood and seeing that he is still in the same position, but awake now, a large and rounded black wetness having appeared in the side of his head. The dog is meandering towards the Grey, whose eye is fixed on the small shape while his ears are revolving back until the line from his nose to their tip is one long arc – a curve that is no longer held above the wood of the enclosure but is slashing downward at the dog, sound quickly bouncing around the barn and the clack of teeth as the Grey strains forward and with repeated stabs tries to bite at the dog, who moves agilely and turns its own head upward with teeth bared, before carrying on its investigation. And this seems to infuriate the Grey because now it is exploding against the wooden wall at its chest, viciously plunging its head and neck towards the ground, desperate for its quarry, its breathing no longer silent and many other sounds now thumping through the barn.

And just a short time ago he was motionless with one leg bent against the other! This thing that he does, of trying to catch the dog with his teeth, is not unexpected, is not something he hasn't done before, yet I still cannot help but watch, my attention held, leaning with the tip of a horn against my own enclosure and feeling the bones in my neck begin to twist. There have been other horses who have lived in the barn, but this is the only one I have seen try and strike at the dog in this way. I used to think that it was because the blood flowed higher in him; it pounds up around his ears whereas the others' hearts could hardly fill their heads – but now I think that this fight in him, this futile movement and sound, comes from somewhere in his mind, a part of it that has grown like fungus in the darkness of this barn that he seldom leaves, fed by the stench of urine and waste that must constantly scrape away at the velvet of his nose and then further up his eye: that glistening orb above the beautiful curve of cheek – I look into that blackness now that the dog has gone and the head has stopped bobbing madly and I see that it is blank, that the Grey does not really know why sweat is now matting the hairs of its flanks.

I push a little with my horn and feel the solidity of the wood as I step back from the barrier, the ache that has gathered in my neck quickly lifting. I do not want to see the Grey as he is now, standing there unmoving, his eyes bulging from his beautiful head, but a wildness curling off him like steam or smoke – a wildness that isn't the thing I see in the creatures that come at night to the edge of the paddock either by accident or curiosity, staring up at me with their tiny iridescent eyes. It is evident in their movements and how they feel the ground beneath them that they have never been touched by man. It is more like a scent – something that can be sensed streaking through the moist air of the barn as if beaten along by the noise that often goes with it: the repetitive banging of metal against wood as the Grey, facing away from me and moving as the sound does, manipulates a heavy object against the far wall, mindlessly, tirelessly, as if he will only stop when his hooves have grown to curl around themselves.

It is the wildness that exists in him doing this and other things that makes me look away – not the savagery in his gallop with ears flat back and hind hooves flashing behind him at the wind. But even as I turn and move a few small steps into my stall I know that soon I will be pressed against the wood again with an ache in my neck, because this thing has a power to make me return to it stronger than all the aversion it provokes and, even now, it is as if my insides have all already turned and are merely awaiting the outer layers to follow. My eyes have spun in their sockets and look through the double darkness of flesh and gloom to where the Grey stands in its repulsiveness, the effortless fluidity from the creature of beautiful head and stone-cracking hooves, diminished to its present coiling stench of madness. This is the thing that attracts me, that makes me enslaved to its observation.

Then the vagueness of the far wall of the barn away from the horse – the thing I am really looking at – is sharpened with light and I know that the barn door has been opened behind me. There is an imaginary silence, like the moment just before a shot bird begins to tumble from its natural flight, and then I hear the Grey turn and the sound of my own hooves reorganising themselves as I too make a line from my hips to my head towards the light. In it stands the boy, a clear shape with the soft grey of aged first-light and the outside world behind him, paused a few steps into the barn and sloping towards the side of him that holds the tangle and curve of what he carries on his arm. He is looking at the Grey, while the horse has turned away, to see him only with a single eye. I move forward quietly, silently maybe, but these two would not hear me now if I snorted because they are joined together, the one looking at the other, the boy full of nervousness that even now is working its way up into his mouth for him to chew on, making ripples under the skin at the sides of his face. But higher, in his gaze, there seems to be an absence of his apprehension or the anger that goes with it, and in this low clear light the colour of his eyes is dimmed but none of their intent – their admiration for the Grey – which masks everything else and is pulling the two together, the boy taking a tentative step forward and in response an ear, a wetness in his direction.

The boy's foot makes a noise as it falls and a shiver passes through the Grey, the slight sound of a hoof being moved on beaten earth quickly followed by moans from the boy – entreaties, the beginning of a courtship as his free hand slowly rises from his side. The boy takes another step and the Grey's neck stiffens, the long head held high over the fencing as if forced up and back with wiring, or by reins, and the boy seeing this pauses as the same stiffness invades him to make his next step smaller, his tall body beginning to crouch as if he might slip beneath the horse's senses, while the sounds he offers become softer and longer, from deeper within his chest.

It appears to be successful, this courtship, and I stand in my own stall watching the boy approach the horse as if the thing that exists between them is solid, a bank of rock that he must climb across with his limbs at full stretch and sweat darkening him. The boy has draped the saddle he is carrying over the fencing between him and the Grey and now his hand is no longer rising in communication but slowly drifting towards the rivulets of vein and flesh near the horse's eye, a clear sign, still an entreaty but a softening now in the boy himself. I look at the gaze that is fixed on the stone-like neck and head he is about to touch and see that it is not something going from the boy to the horse, but a drinking, a needful suckling that flows the other way. The Grey must feel the boy's breaths as too warm; he too must hear the panting sound they make coming from a blood-flushed throat.

His hand has landed on the grey neck, only to lift off and

land again more firmly, repeatedly, until the sound of a loud patting is in the barn. The boy has straightened and is slowly filling with the swagger that usually pilots him – his body is no longer marking the air around it with signs of his fear and inhibition but is moving outward, like a plant or weed growing, filling the space around him until his presence is towering above us again. The movements, the noises he makes are those of triumph and a creature with lightness in its feet. And in my stall I think how I have watched such growth in my paddock, marked the appearance of every tiny leaf and the stretching of all the translucent stalks that they sprout from – and then when they are high enough, just as they seem to pause before releasing the small buds further upward a hoof becomes their cloud and the whole thing is back in the ground and broken – a mess of sap and thorn. I am against my stall's boundary as I think this, feeling the wood give in the earth quietly as I push into it, watching the boy, watching his youth crackle out of him to prick at the air around us with its thistles.

A silent movement, as quick as one of the skeletal orange cats that slink through the fencing, and the Grey has brought his head to the side, his neck curving, no longer stone, and is swivelling the mouth with its receding black lips round to the boy's arm. In the same movement the horse's teeth appear – no hesitation, no separation of intent between him getting near the boy and biting him and now he has the boy's shirt in his teeth and is pulling it to widen and distort the line from shoulder to hand. The boy has made a noise high in pitch like as he did when he was small, and has stepped with a little hop away from the stall, rubbing at his arm, hunching and looking back at the Grey. I can see that the boy is afraid now, but that his faith has not been crushed because he is soon moving back towards the horse, his arm raised in front of him while the noises he makes, the cooing noises, though still supplicating, now have a rough and tearing edge of anger. The Grey has raised his head sharply but his ears are askew, neither pricked forward nor flattened back and I think that his mind has wandered after the perfunctory lunge of teeth at the boy, and that he will soon have the saddle on his back, the metal in his mouth.

And in a short while the boy is also calmer. Now he has one hand on the taut grey flesh of neck. The other has felt for the bridle and is lifting it from the stall's fence. The anger has gone from his voice and now there really is a thickness to it – a warmth as if his heart is forcing all his blood through its air to moisten it before reaching the horse's ear, which the boy, bending forward and looking upward, has taken into his hand to squeeze and stroke, a smooth movement becoming slower in repetition, but a hungry one, as if his hand was a mouth. Their heads are very close together and are going to touch – I watch as the two covered skulls drift together like minuscule flotsam does in my trough – a gentle bump and the closing of the horse's eye, and although the boy's are hidden I imagine them wide and staring and brimming with it: the happiness, the thing that can be smelt and seen in him as clearly as if it were another animal in the barn.

He and the Grey, now resting against each other like foals! But it should not be a surprise to me, because the boy remains the same in this – his hunger to be close to the horse is constant. That is what I see in him every morning I am in the barn and he appears, framed by the different colours behind him – while it is the Grey, changing, twisted one way and another by his rotting mind, who shuns this contact and makes it a rare occurrence. The touching of heads, the milking of an ear, must happen in the boy's hopes every time he opens the barn door, and yet it seldom comes about – for both of us – that he can be smelling the rich and sweet smell of the

Grey so keenly while I, a few paces distant, can watch hungrily, but merely with a stomach for the event between them.

The boy's other hand has abandoned the bridle, leaving it draped on the fence where it rests and then slithers quietly to the ground. Neither of them notices it fall and I watch it coiling on the ground with a glint of metal as it slips. Then, looking up, I see that the boy has got the Grey's nose in one hand, his ear in the other, and he is feeling the whiskers and passing his touch over the warm apertures of the huge nostrils. It has begun at the bottom of the long head and is working its way up the ridge of bone towards the flat space between the eyes. He is almost there when the Grey, his eye opening slowly, suddenly bucks his head up and bites the boy on the soft underside of his arm. The boy screams and pushes away from horse and stall, staggering backward, bringing the bitten arm in close to his body and arching his back over so that he faces the ground. He is silent save for his breaths that are being sucked in quickly and forcing the only movement of his body. Then he moans and shakes his head, more breathing, another moan and a violent movement of the head as if it is gripped and he tries to free it. And when he begins to take a few steps, still bent over, I hear the Grey stamping at the ground and look up to see him shifting in his stall – as if they mimic the other's movement.

But the boy does not remain hunched for long, and now he has stood up and is stepping resolutely down the space between our stalls, away from us both. We watch him recede and become unclear in the gloom, our necks having turned in unison. Then he is beyond what I can see, my vision blocked by the sides of my stall, so I turn to the Grey who still watches him, ears pricked towards the end of the barn that for me is hidden, has always been unseen. There is another small shuffle of hoof on earth and I watch what must be the boy's return flicker through the Grey, one ear revolving towards the door and the light. I twist my head against its confines, feeling the tip of a horn pushing into the old rotting wood and this way I can see the boy as well, walking quickly back towards the Grey, the fur above his eyes jutting forward and the thing he holds behind his back confirming what I thought I heard – the sound of a piece of wood being pulled from a stack of many. He holds it so that one end is at his back, the other brushes the back of his leg, down where it bends. It is thin – far thinner than his wrist that is twisted disagreeably to hide it, so much so that looking at it I can feel the pain – the ache that such an effort would cause and for a moment I am fascinated by this, sucked in by this unexpected salience, and I watch as the tendons in that wrist relax and the arm drops, the stick twisting and then rising and beginning to cut the air audibly, flashing out to the side at the end of a straightened arm before slashing back inward and down to hit the Grey.

The horse sees the last part of the stick's journey and has begun to step backward and avert his head, but even so it meets some of the large area of his skull, making a flat cracking sound – the unmistakable sound of beaten bone, muffled by the flesh around it. The Grey jumps backward, his mane furling and rippling and a breath taken that could be either inward or out, and the boy deftly gains a foothold on the stall's fence, pulling himself up so that he can lean over the barrier and swing the stick high over his head to strike at the Grey again, who rears a bit and flashes a hoof, his dark eyes bulging and the veins suddenly pulled up to the surface of his skin to cover his face like a cobweb. The boy cannot reach him any more but still swipes the stick through the air, his shouts disconnected from his movements, the horse now pressed against the back of his stall stamping and flinching, his head held low and then high, looking for a space he can get to where the brute, the vessel of ugly youth with its slashing stick and screaming will not be.

Even if the Grey and I were in the same herd – as it seems this roof and these walls try to force us to be through repetition – I would not hear the creak of wood as much as I do now, or feel the scrape and cling of the earth at the base of the long thick posts I press against. There is something in me, watching the boy and the horse, listening to the hiss of the stick diminish and become less frequent, that locks me in so that I cannot turn away – I am chained and pulled so that my own broad snout must face this scene, this thing that is like a fire in the barn, eating away at the walls and the beams. And I should be enlivened, I should feel the air bursting into every part of my lungs as I breathe quietly and watch, but even now I stamp at the ground because I do not feel this – there is no excitement or pleasure in the fire I see, and stronger is the dread of its effect – I worry for the walls and the beams, the fragile posts that hold up the fences because I do not want them destroyed or altered. Others may have put up these barriers, but I have made them with what I have put within them, and while I am engrossed with this fight between the Grey and the boy, I despise the sickness in my stomach and the twitching of forgotten, distant muscles that it triggers.

The boy has climbed over into the stall and has the bridle in his hand. Both of them move up and down jerkily with their breaths, but their aspects – their tired aspects and earth-pointed eyes – declare a mutual unwillingness to fight. The boy makes his noises and raises his arm; the Grey flashes his head out to the side in a compact little movement and a flap of lips and then they are in contact again, a hand on the metallic coat – hairs that must already be mired in the thick and oily sweat I can smell and see in patches of darker grey on the high flank. And then the aim of all this, the reason the boy is here in the barn, is suddenly in front of the horse's nose and being slipped over his head, the metal entering his mouth with a sound that truly frightens, a soft clinking quickly silenced that travels down my ear into a place inside me that is like the end of the barn where the boy got the stick – unseen, unlit by eyes that cannot turn there.

The boy is lifting the reins over the Grey's head, and as I watch them land on the long neck, my own twitches and I scrape the fencing with my horn. The sound isn't loud but it seems to remind them both of the tumult they halved between them; the horse jerks a little and the boy turns to look at me, as if realising for the first time that he is being, and has been, watched. His head is twisted and angled and obscured by his shoulder, but in his bright eyes – the little evening suns he carries in his small skull to try and wilt all he looks at – there is a glimmer I recognise, a fear, the same thing I see in the dogs' eyes and shoulders the moment before they are shouted at or beaten.

And now I must turn away and face the wall of the barn where I will not see them, where I won't see the little movements and flickers of limb and mane of their ritual that I can still hear going on behind me, another muscle twitching distantly as I imagine hands on the grey flank, the sudden cling of the saddle, the weightier pats of the boy's recovering belief. They seldom touch me, they never touch me, whereas the Grey is mauled and suddenly pulled out of the barn and into the light after being left to rot in darkness for days, his life swinging from a quiet madness to bright violence – a violence of which he is a part and perhaps even the beginning – and I wonder if he does not enjoy fighting with the boy, if he doesn't dream of him every time he is banging the piece of metal at the back of his stall, grinding the space between when he is alone and when they come to saddle him down to nothing. I step deeper into my stall and, seeing the smeared undulations of its far wall, suddenly I want to lower my head and smash it because I find that I envy the Grey. I want to feel what he does – the crushing, putrid boredom suddenly released in the eluding of blows in the barn, or better and rarer the moments he has to himself in the paddock, where his spirit surfaces and I watch as he crashes from one end of his enclosure to another, looking like all the noble history of his breed, full of a life I fear I have never felt. All this he has while I, unmolested, fed and watered, am content to take the things I see in the paddock with me back into the safety of the barn, where I am left undisturbed to make of them what I choose.

A squeaking behind me and then the sound of shod hooves on the hard floor, their rhythm clipped and not the Grey's own and I know he is being tugged by his mouth out of the stall, out of the barn and into the morning, the clopping fading behind me. I imagine the two as they walk along – the Grey seemingly acquiescent and the boy leading him, feeling the power of the thing next to him through the irregular slacking and tightening of the reins he pulls – the horse rippling his mane, clearing his nostrils. I cannot be led like this, being only ever pushed by the dull impulses that prod me forward, like hunger to make me wander over to the dried grass, or thirst to cause the weight of my head to drop down towards the trough. And sometimes it is like a sharp pain in me to hear the horse being led like that – not for him or his slavishly lowered head, or for the boy, but for something I cannot grasp before the pain has gone.

CHAPTER 3

Through the wall of the barn I can hear noises – the boy's footsteps followed by a scraping noise of wood against the stony earth, then a colder sound like a hiss that I know to be metal. There is more scraping of wood and suddenly lines of bright white appear in the darkness at the back of my stall. I take a few steps forward, towards this occurrence that I see most days, that I wait for eagerly and dread at the same time so that it means nothing, this opening of the door – it means nothing as I lower my head and walk to the large opening, feeling my dormant flesh slapping and twisting around my thick bones, the distant twitching of muscles immediately silenced by this greater movement. The sun is hidden but the sky still bright enough to blind me as my head breaks out from the darkness, and I am mostly past him when I see the boy at my side, standing behind the fence, with the rope that he used to pull the big door open still in his hand.

His eyes aren't on me and having hunted for their gaze with a slightly turned neck I brush the pillar at my other side, part of the opposite fence that means I cannot turn, that forces me ahead along the rutted channel of wood railing to my paddock, or a slow uncertain backing into the barn. And I find that I do not mind that I cannot turn – I don't mind that I plod forward with uneven bars and slats so close at my flanks, that my shoulders brush one side and then the other. The boy has caught up and is walking beside me, his head down, watching the ground ahead of him as he follows the line of fencing, his thin hand occasionally rising to pat at the posts. The channel has been turning and then after a sharper twist I see the paddock opening out ahead; for an instant a sliver of fear touches me like a quiet sound, but entering the paddock I find it has not changed, that it does not change beyond what I can consume.

I enter the space, my head emerging into it as it did into the light, and then I turn to look at the boy behind me, watching as he reaches over to close the gate that will block off the channel. Another slow swing of my neck, feeling the weight of my head crossing from one foreleg to the other, a tiny sound coming from the pressured hoof beneath my snout, and then I am looking into the other paddock, where the Grey stands near the fence, attached to it by the reins that arc below his mouth. His head rises and turns, his neck making a wonderful curve of stone that only the delicacy of his pointed ears betrays, and thinking that he must look to the house I trample the ground over to the fence, stopping when I can see more of the bright white walls, the blocks of green and sudden dotted colours of the gardens.

There is movement at one of the sharp borders on the ground where the flat grass gives way to duller earth: a figure has taken a first step from one to the other, arms clad in bright white rising away from the torso, the small squat head of shining pink jolting down to the side as balance is lost and then regained. Beneath the white of the chest and arms the legs are jet black, a sudden thinning and tapering downward to the knee where the blackness changes to another that shines, even in this clouded but already hot morning. I watch as the man approaches, dazzled by the white and the black, a stark shape sticking out from both the house and the landscape and taking small steps towards us as if pulled by our gazes – me, the horse and the boy – and I know that they are watching as I do because the noises, the scrapes and shuffles have stopped behind me where the boy is, and the horse has not turned his head.

Now the man is a few steps away from the fence that runs in a long line facing the house, and through the wire I can see his head and thick neck emerging, then the band of dark hair starting above his ear and curling around the back of his skull to end above the other ear, and the glistening pink-brown at the very top of his head. He is clumsy in his movements, his legs making too much upward travel before stretching over the ground – a waste in this heat – while his short, thick arms are held almost stiffly at his sides. But his aspect – his gait is one that gives me a quiet pleasure and I stand quietly to watch him as he comes to the fence and leans a stubby arm on one of the posts, rests his eye briefly on me and then calls gruffly to the boy. I hear the boy answer from behind me, a higher voice than the one he uses with either me or the Grey, and then his footsteps are coming around the curve of the paddock, his form entering into my vision from the side, passing through one eye to another and joining the man so that both are in front of me, one short and rounded, the other elongated and with a stiffness in his bearing that tries to hide his youth.

They turn away from me and I watch as they walk together to the gate that opens into the Grey's enclosure. I can hear their voices, the man's even lower now but clear over the crunching of their feet, and the boy's gradually returning to its original timbre, away from the higher wavering of when he first answered his elder. Their voices respond to each other for the whole time that they walk along the fence, and continue to do so when the boy peels away and leans with both arms on the gatepost, the man bending over the gate, his hands moving until it swings open with a soft squeak.

I lift and turn my head to look at the Grey, who stands motionless, watching the man walk up to him, his ears tuned forward to the squat little creature's awkward steps – yet with none of the desperate interest in his eye or the deceitful blankness beneath their surface that he showed for the boy, or even the small dog, before flying at them both. I hear him snort – a soft sound of welcome that ends with the quietest of whinnies, which I doubt the man or boy can hear – and as the man raises his hand to grip the ridge between nose and eyes the Grey's ears go askew and he pushes his weight forward into his front legs, pressing against the man's hand firmly to gently collapse his arm, making the white and black figure stagger a little and emit a sound of reproach, of greeting. There is a sound to my side and I angle my head and see that the boy is shifting a little against his post, his face passive as he looks into the paddock, but his foot working away at the soil at its base.

I turn back and see that the man has disappeared behind the horse, who is taking little dancing steps without really moving, and through whose light grey legs I can see those of the man: shining black sticks also hopping about with weight in one and then the other. Then these sticks are pulled upward and I look to the horse's back where the man has appeared, his face twisted and his eyes bulging, breaths whistling out of him as he clambers into the saddle and sweat glistening all over his head. Over comes the black leg to find the stirrup, the foot working into the metal as if spurred by the glinting at its heel, and the man leans forward over the horse's neck, pulling the reins to him, shifting his weight in saddle and leg while the Grey shifts and dances, his tail rising with a flick that curls its end.

Then the man straightens his back and both man and horse begin to fade. As they walk away from where I stand close to the boy they disappear as separate things, fusing quickly into a single beast of movement and stillness, the Grey's neck curving downward to rest on the thing in his mouth, his legs and hooves moving slowly and fluidly in an exaggerated trot while above this, above the rhythm of the softly clapped-at ground there is nothing but solidity – from the horse's flank to the top of the man's angled, listening head – there is no looseness between them, no sign that one is different from the other. I see bright black move back against the grey flank and they slide from a trot into a slow, loping canter, the augmented horse's beautiful form now pushing out grace of movement towards me in a torrent, a thick flow in the air that makes my breathing shallow and the blood struggle to my head. I watch this thing circle the paddock, hearing the compact rhythmic breaths as it passes where I stand, feeling unsteady and afraid for my own balance in the glare of what I see – as if by watching I am being sucked towards them into the fusion they have become – adding to the bond as the boy does with his eyes.

But the pulling is weakened when the man reveals himself by calling to the boy, his image as something separate materialising high above so that I must strain my neck upward, his voice breaking the cord that an instant before I thought would pull my nose into sharp wire. The boy replies uncertainly; the man answers loudly and then suddenly his body stiffens and pulses a command down into the horse, and as they lope quickly to the far end of the paddock away from us they begin to merge again, a single entity leaning sharply in a tight turn, a structure that moves up from the dust-kicking hooves to split into two spines like the branches of a tree, the rapt, bud-like growths of its heads bowing softly together in the same wind.

Now this thing has turned, small and distant, and faces the boy where he stands near the closed gate. There is a quick dance of hooves before a lowering and a surge forward that settles to a fast canter, the sound of hooves becoming sharper and threatening on the hard ground, and suddenly I feel as if I am something small and wild in the sun-dried woods, hearing the crackling of fire. I watch and can feel the boy watching, as if his sight forms bars through the air – solid things that perhaps would want to stop the thing powering towards us, would want to spear the chests and slash at their eyes as they loom in his vision that is filled with a completeness he desires but hasn't achieved, must feel he can never achieve as they arrive and the long grey forelegs curl up before him towards the horse's chest, the already set hind legs pushing the beast into the air, a sudden silence as the earth is left and falls away beneath the arcing shape, the top of the fence trying to scuff the hooves that pass over it but failing and the boy so close to the flying mass of flesh that I fear he will reach out and touch it. Then the legs straighten, opening unnoticeably like petals, and they land on the other side of the fence, the spines and heads bending a little closer to each other as the ground shudders into them, before this intrusion is overcome and the canter is collected – another tight turn and a shout and a snort, a flash from each of them as if they must separate momentarily to release their glory.

And in this moment, where his voice still seems attached to his open mouth, the man looks at me and I see myself, standing near the fence, a dull heavy thing that does not leave the ground, that clings to it desperately like a tree and changes little more than a tree from year to year. In the instant the man sees me I can feel his contempt, a moment of loathing for me as quick and brief as his exultation. As he suddenly sees me standing there watching him I must become for him everything that he has just made the gesture of leaving behind – the annual lazy adding of flesh like a tree its rings, the lack of movement, the corners of my stance that will not pierce any direction unless I will it – he must see these things and in the same way that I will look at the stars he now looks at me and crafts his own edifice of what I am, filling my skin with his own blood that he would be rid of, pinning to me the traits of the unmalleable, the uncompliant, the things that stubbornly remain, like a cluster of dark memories in his mind.

I turn from this, feeling the great weight in my hooves pushing into the ground as I move away from the fence – only to find another in my paddock, the small dog of earlier with nose down, pursuing its scents amongst my hoof prints and the few remaining weeds staggering upward from the earth. Then the ground is moving beneath me, the warm air rushing around the tips of my horns, my legs suddenly whipping over the ground and the hooves crushing stone and clod because they must move downward too – and when I am almost on the white and brown shape of the canine I lower my head, watching as the dog, large and intricately detailed this close to my eye, springs neatly to the side and away from the tip of a long horn. I turn sharply and strike forward, aiming for where I saw it last, but again it evades me, turning in an impossibly tight arc and then running, heading for the hole in the fence through which it came while I follow, joining its path as it straightens, trying to scoop it off the ground with one horn and then another, dust and grit from its tiny and impudent paws jumping up at my nose and eyes. But I stop far from the fence, giving up the foolish chase to watch the dog lower itself and push through the gap, while I am left standing, feeling blood and breath pulse in me, the heat cloying, a thing suddenly pressing at me from all sides so that I fear my skin will become dry like the earth and rupture. What have I destroyed, what have I altered with this recklessness? I turn to face the ground I have just trodden, seeing instantly a myriad broken stems, growing structures that I have nurtured through scrutiny, destroyed prematurely – and even the cracks in the ground that fence them, that hold one thought back from another, these have been smudged and lessened by my hooves. And the man and the boy – vague and uninteresting shapes at the top edge of my downward-pointed vision – I can hear their voices intertwining, running together like birdsong or water.

CHAPTER 4

Every day that I am left in the paddock, every time that I am
not enticed back into the barn with the scent of feed, this is
the moment I wait for, as if the whole day of heat and little
movement, of staring from one end to another, has merely been
a prelude – an emptiness before the sky begins to turn a deeper
shade of blue, the sun sitting on the horizon mute and reddening,
bright still but merely pawing at my eye. I look up to the thick-
ening blue, watching the darkness creep down from above and
waiting for the moment; then slowly they begin to appear, illusory as if doubts, first the one point of light around which all
the others circle, followed by a few more that I dot around the
sky – but then what I have begun slips from my command and
they emerge so fast and numerous that I can only watch quietly,
my neck beginning to ache, my breathing the tiniest whisper
of movement, and the sight above flowing into my head and
chest so that I feel as if I am running.

The hot day around me has vanished, replaced by the thick smell of night, and I can feel the heat leaving my body, spilling from it so that I am relieved as if I have been burdened, my limbs and shoulders losing the rigidity the sun forced into them. I am free to drop my head and move forward and turn, a crackle of stones beneath my hooves, the air a wonderful thing to move through. Do I imitate the horse, in these sporadic trots forward? Maybe I hope to capture a sliver of his spirit, his poison, to feel it running down my tendons to tighten the muscles that lurch and shift sloppily around my bones – to imagine that I too am a thing like him. But then I think that I do not want any part of him in me, anything that might block my path to the things I see above and around me. I am content with a little movement forwards, a light skimming of hooves over the stones and hard earth, to stop and have energy still to lift my head and hold it there.

A sound pulls my gaze away from the horizon, the sound of light paws on the earth behind me: I think it is the dog, in my paddock again, and I turn to meet this renewed intrusion, moving more quickly in the cooler air, feeling the litheness of night in my limbs, and then I am turned with head and horns raised to see nothing within the fence except the weeds in the

dusk, some broken and showing the trail of my earlier pursuit. But beyond the paddock, loping heavily and almost silently is another thing – a canine shape undulating towards me as it pads up to the fence, a large body above large paws, the broad head appearing behind the wire with thick flanges dropping from its snout on either side, an excess of ears and lips making the eyes, alive with a soft glinting as they watch me, seem dwarfed within the skull.

Seldom do I see this head so close, rather than a distant shape on the ground, the end of a body slumped in the sun near the white walls of the house. And looking into the small eyes, at the broad space between them and the thick snout down to the nose, I am reminded of the image that looks up at me from water, while the body of the dog, seen now from the front, the

hind end hidden behind the mass of chest, thick neck and shoulder – this is like when the boy looks at me and I see these things reflected in his eyes. Except that there is a difference: between our forms there is a difference beyond the shape of our teeth or our size and that runs to something deeper, as if one were made of stone and the other of mud.

Suddenly the dog finishes its short scrutiny and its head drops to snuffle and snort at the ground near the fence. Behind it the house becomes visible, glowing a pale blue and surrounded by the deeper blue and black shadow caused by the brightness of the moon. The sky is now almost black, the stars have emerged and a myriad brilliant points are already making shapes that I can feel swirling and forming above me so that I want to look upward, as if something is pulling at me, hooks inside my skull and in the sockets of my eyes. But with the presence of the dog – even though it ignores me, equally rapt within its world of scents – I can't and suddenly it strikes me that the dog's proximity contains a maliciousness – not of intent but from the rareness of its company, an event that is blocking me from my own intent and that herds the little warmth left on the surface of my skin down into the flesh of my neck.

I think that I will step forward and snort, when something shimmers at the wall of the house beyond – a soft, curved movement impossible from its hard white sides so that for a moment I think it is my sight that has pulled it from the stone, an echo of the movement of stars in the black above. But this vision, this shape emerges further as I look, a small pale figure sluicing away from the paleness behind it, the angle of limbs mostly hidden beneath moon-drenched cloth, and it is not until the thing is crossing the patch of grass that I can detect the movement of legs, the slightest swinging of arms at the waist and lastly the head with its long dark hair, shining in the half-light so that now I can see it all – the separate things of arm and the skin of thin neck above the glowing fabric quickly shaping into the girl of the house, stepping lightly as she goes, making no sound as she walks down to where I stand perfectly still with head raised watching this little creature of the twilight, marking her progress, interested as she stumbles on a stone when she leaves the smoothness of the grass, confused when the blunt head sprouts like a growth at her side before understanding it is the other large dog, kin of the one that is already at the fence.

And as she gets closer still, shadowed by the hound that carries far more flesh on its frame, I catch a scent like that of crushed flowers, as if her small feet have dragged some of the garden down into the scrub and rocky earth and this smell pulls something down inside me so that I wonder if I have staggered where I stand – faint and mixed memories tugging at my chest of when I was younger, with sharper bones at my shoulder and hind, bones stroked and squeezed by a miniature hand through the gaps in the small wooden stall, the same hand now a little longer and wider that rises to grip the wire of the fence between us. But then, in the stall and at other times, she had the man behind her, his voice loud and disturbing the soft concentrated rhythm of her breaths – and suddenly he would grab her by the waist and lift her over the top of the stall so that she looked down at me, a long black shape in the straw with the sharp and sweet smell of milk in my nostrils, slowly accumulating the flesh that swills around my maturity, and I would look up to her eyes and see in their large grey glaze a disturbance, a half-formed hunger that I saw was in her and felt in my own stomach, though it churned fully with what was in it.

Seeing her now, clutching at the fence with her still tiny hand, I am reminded of the changes I have wrought in her face – the slight widening and lengthening of chin and cheek, the rising of the flat pale space above her eyes before the darker curve of long black hair. She watches me, her eyes glinting in my direction, fuller than the vague interest of the dog and keener given that they cannot resort to the scents beneath. And I have no compulsion to stamp or turn my head away because her presence provokes little in me but half-believed memories, thoughts recalled of warm light, soft hay beneath and a small figure draping herself half-into my stall, her voice quiet but insistent, her arm reaching through the gaps in the wood to swab at my side like the tongue of a snake – not a thing that I recoiled from but neither one that I leaned towards despite the sensations it produced in the skin and in the growing flesh beneath, always aware of her eyes watching me and the thing behind them, the thing like an illness making their blinking infrequent and heavy.

The other dog that was at her flank now turns and begins with head down to waddle along the fence so that she is left standing alone, but with a hound of muscle and jaw either side of her a small distance away as if ordered. She has one arm linked through the barred metal gate of the paddock, the other with fingers hooked on the thinner wire. The freer arm makes a movement towards me and then away so that I am pulled forward, stepping slowly to her, undiscouraged by the small whimper-like sounds dissipating from her nostrils. As I get nearer a strand of wire cuts across her eyes to disfigure them, and when they reappear above it rising from this thinnest of horizons I feel a caution and a warning rattle from somewhere within me, as if the wire has scraped a layer from her eyes so that I am able to see more clearly the thing in them that must be a sickness, or the sign of one like a stench: a writhing confusion that is there for an instant but that she blinks away with slow lids and a slight nodding of the head.

Now I am at the fencing, smelling her cautiously, flinching as her hand passes through the bars of the heavy gate to flit above my head like a bat or insect. A few more compressions of the earth beneath me and I have my shoulder pressed against the gate, feeling the long bars pushing across the flesh there with a weak warmth, hearing a quiet clicking as the metal takes my weight and can go no further. The girl has stepped back but I can see her even with my head averted, a white shape in the corner of my eye appearing like a crescent as she creeps around the curve of my haunch, her breathing regular and clear and intensifying as she approaches the dark flesh framed in the bars – and I think that I feel the heat of her hand before she touches me – then her fingers landing and scraping along my skin to send ripples of feeling into my flesh, my eyes half closing and my breaths stopped to silence myself before this, to stand motionless and allow the thing inside me to suckle from these fingers, to drink from the sudden disturbance at my skin. Her fingers travel further and then stop to become a sharpness, an edge like the beak of a bird picking at where the blood flowed and then hardened in one of the small holes of my shoulder – they dig and lever away at this hardness until I feel it lift and tear off to release an almost imperceptible wetness, like finding the smell of water beneath an overturned stone.

Then the dog that I can see, a shape dulled and incomplete with my attention being led in slow circles by the fingers at my shoulder, quickly raises a part of itself and barks, a short sound urgently echoed by the other one to make a noise as if a calling bird has flown low and massive across the ground. The fingers spring from my skin and I step into the paddock to raise my head, to lift the horns so that they point at the mass of stars and black above – and I see that both the dogs are alert and looking towards the house, their thick trunks and legs arranged so that their own broad heads and intent are leaning in the same direction – and looking to the fading glow of the house I can see nothing in the night air until a figure suddenly appears on the scrub, having already left the grass undetected, dark and whipping the air with tiny movements of hand, head, neck and ankle so that I feel the blood in me flow upward to throb at my eyes and ears – a stamping sound from beneath my snout and breath flying from it to spray the air, the girl spinning quickly in this mist to face away from me.

Without slowing the approaching figure emits an angry sound and the tension in the dogs drops from them heavily, as if something has been taken from them, a disappointment as they recognise their master. As he gets closer, his feet punching crisply at the ground, the girl seems to shrink in the fabric that covers her, the thin spine curving and her shoulders with their shifting covering of thick black hair rising to try and hide her head. I hear her voice, high and quiet, stuttering at first before flowing steadily towards the man that she faces, but this sound is met and dispersed by another coming from the shifting figure in the moonlight, now only a few paces away, still walking quickly down to the paddock and shimmering in and out of the scrub and the moonlight, his paler face and hairless crown prominent and occasionally unattached to his black-covered body, a flying head that now spits a hushed stream of anger towards the girl to make her silent and cower further.

Now he is on her and raises an arm – the movement and muffled crack of fabric triggers my head to shudder – and I think he will strike out like a cat and he does, but lightly and not to hit her but to fuse his hand to her arm. He bends his body to bring his face to hers, the breath and voice of his anger spitting at her, flowing from his arm into hers so that limply she is buffeted, trying to recoil from him but shaken out of this want at the point that they are joined. I watch as his head turns, the muscles stretched and rising in his throat and neck so that he can put his eyes on me, guided by a straight arm that he looks down and that is pointed in my direction. And even in this dim light, through the thickness of his anger I see myself in flashes across his eyes, as if looking at something in the flickering lightning of a storm – a huge black body part-framed by gate and fence, held behind this structure, but at the same time, the heavy curvature of skull and horns bursting above it. Then his head revolves away and his attention is back on the girl, whose own thin high voice can be heard intermittently, the man shaking her to resume his angry growling that continues but is lessening, dying as the girl's spirit rises, her arm coming up to scrabble at the thick and heavy one that is attached to her, her voice no longer stuttering but pushing back at the man so that he can only offer the occasional grunt.

Her voice stops and the noise they have been making quickly dissipates into the night as if towards silence, and I hear a rustling from one of the dogs: a sound of scratched earth, the parting of vegetation. The two figures are motionless, their heads close together, the girl a curved paleness against the darker man and black earth surrounding them. Then she looks at me, her eyes glistening and the same iridescence on her cheeks below them, and she is thinking of me because again I see myself, a larger shape now towering above the top of the fence, the earth and crushed scrub around me changing to a bright yellow – then a brief explosion of colours: blue and pink figures like birds stalking the substrate as if hunting smaller things, red walls running curved and tightening inward to force these things towards me, constricting us so that their shadows mingle with my own. It is the same thing that I see with the boy, that I share with him, except then he is never present, whereas now the girl exists in this vision, she is a part of it if not its substance. It is her massive and elongated body curled around the red walls that have crushed us together on the dirt and I think that unlike the boy she does not revel in the scene but wants to smother it – to destroy it.

I can feel the blood pulsing in me as I watch this, an instant stretched to the length of a morning, a thing in the girl's mind or my own and one that is suddenly ended as she turns away and arches her back, retreating from the fingers that have jabbed sharply into her stomach. The man's hand is poised at her chest, his voice low and now vicious, and I can feel that the dogs have paused and their attention is also on the figures. I can feel this as clearly as if I could see them both – they too are watching as the fingers dart forward again and the girl cries out as they strike her chest, the man releasing his arm from hers so that she can step back and clutch herself, he waving in my direction in a whip-like movement and his voice still with a dangerous fury, one that she does not dare respond to.

He turns and paces away, feet pattering tightly on the earth, his anger no longer as visible in his movements but still present, and I think that it must have burrowed deeper into him, towards the memories he has of finding her alone in the barn, stroking my flank and feeling the wetness of my nose, cooing at my ungainly form as if I were one of the hounds. Watching him recede I see a stout low shape slink lazily to his side, a companion he ignores despite the broad head angled up to him, but that at other times he often touches with a gentle hand – a hand that has never touched me gently, that is not linked to eyes that could see me as anything other than monstrous: a dark vessel like a pool into which he spits those things his rumination finds distasteful. His anger at the girl must come from this, must be directed at her willingness to touch without hitting, to take the numbness away from the patches of my skin she scratches. He does not mind the boy's stick bouncing from my hind – he does not mind this contact yet he is afraid of her bird-like lightness of touch and I take a step to see him better, to watch as without stopping the man turns and calls back to the girl, the fury still coarse in his voice. I wonder if that is the only thing she hears, or whether her ears can detect the softening within the rebuke, how he wants to bring her closer with the same utterance. But she doesn't follow him and quickly he and the dog are lost from my sight, becoming a vague, liquid shimmering in the darkness before disappearing into it.

The girl remains standing where she is, her head bent forward and a hand rubbing at her chest, then she looks up to me and steps forward to the gate, her eyes wide and staring at me but blank and unrevealing, no vision of myself contained in them, just a strong trace of this sickness I sense in her that makes me feel as if I am watching a lizard or mouse emerging madly to crawl across the path of a cat. I watch the small figure of bone and fabric reach up to the gate and see the slithering of her wrist through the bars, the fingers feeling where her eyes can't like an insect. The metal is resistant, because she appears to hang from it, but horizontally – she tugs sideways at the handle until it breathes into life with a noise that makes the remaining dog snap its head up, a noise jerking and then extended as metal slides through metal and a sound through which I can hear every beat of my heart like a long roll of thunder – nothing moving inside me or outside of my skin that does not seem attached to the thick metal bolt, the thing sliding across my eyes and through my stomach to sicken me, to make me clutch at the air in my lungs.

I hear the man's footsteps on the dark ground and look up,

expecting to see him returning to attach himself to her with renewed anger – but I am startled because it is still the sound of him walking back up to the house, yet he seems closer in his retreat, and I watch as he and the dog at his side disappear again beneath the wash of black. The girl has called and then she too is almost at the house, just visible in her white clothing, a canine outline obscuring her lower half as it crosses her path. I look to the gate where the bolt has been pulled back and she is still there, her hand hovering as it tries to reverse through the angles of metal, turning and slipping at the same time that she lowers her body and swings around to begin walking away. The gate itself has not moved and I stand a body's length from it, motionless, the sky above revolving smoothly and then with a frightening speed – the sounds of lessening footsteps, of the girl's call to the dog and the quiet slide of the metal in my ears and in my skull, a herd of sounds, a single sound and I think that I have been frozen to where I stand and the sky must soon lighten above me.

But the stars have not moved more than a day's growth of grass, and the girl is only now disappearing into an aperture of the house. It is still the same part of the night and I am not fixed and can take a hesitant step towards the gate, slowly parting the air, feeling it slip along my flanks and beneath my belly. There is something in the earth I stand on that I can feel pushing its way upward and that I am trying to hold down with all the weight in my hooves. Some of it escapes and fires into my shoulders and down along my spine, twitching the muscles slung around the bone to tighten them, making the air a solid thing that I can feel at the tip of my horns. I am pulled forward, scuffing the ground with a hoof, staring at the gate and its bolt – while the sky above, the thing that sustains me more than the stalks in my trough, it is lifting away as if the eye that has watched me, has scorned me and crushed me, is closing.

CHAPTER 5

I can hear the sweet air of night swirling into my nostrils, the smell that seems to rise from the earth, thick and intoxicating, travelling down my snout and into the back of my skull as if it is the thing that holds my limbs to my spine, the force that binds me to the ground which tries to shift and buck my weight from it, and that holds the fence with its gate to the earth. The gate I stare at is now a part of me as much as a heartbeat or a breath. And yet my breaths have now become shallow, no longer a mindless movement of air but an event, a thing my thoughts must wrap around instead of leaking towards the bolt of the gate, which I cannot see in the darkness but know has moved, has been slid back to perhaps a point where it is open.

And if it is open, if I am to lower my head and push against it to feel no resistance except its thinly hanging weight, what will I become? The thing from the ground, the excitement that pulsates from there and out from my spine into the furthest, most dimly felt parts of my flesh, is not lessening but beginning to rage, as if each attentive breath I pull inward feeds it, spreads it so that it begins to lick around my skull like a hot sickness, the dying of a disease within me, the pleasure of a lifting pain as the prospect of freedom, novel and untrodden, rises like the sun – but a sun trapped in a sky that I hold down with my hooves, that is mine to cross its blackness.

Has it always been there, this urge, this desire that now shimmers in me? I feel my heart pounding, but not because I have forced my mass quickly across the ground, not because I am standing and fighting for the first breaths after some futile movement. It beats as if trying to blast the scabs from my shoulders, to make the blood spurt from these former holes and release the thing that wants to push me forward and through the gate, but which I press down and try to restrain, part through unwillingness but also to feel: to remain quiet and witness this prospect as it blooms in me. It must have always existed: a mostly silent but ever-present contempt for the fences, and the wood that holds me in my stall – and before where I thought it a film, a flashing slime covering my thoughts, now in its fruition I fear it has been the basis, the beginning and foundation of what I should be and what I have tried to smother with a skyward gaze, the watching of the small things around me.

I lift a single hoof and move it forward so that my mass is pitched slightly towards the gate, a jerking impulse, a single spark from the fire that is giving the night a phantom hotness. Even this small gesture, the crunching of ground well-trodden, has a shocking newness, as if my legs that haven't moved are poles driven in the ground, anchoring me to the paddock that I know – and this one footfall towards the gate an imbalance, an action that will destroy what I have made, the things I have held with my eyes and the memories trapped behind them.

Because it is like fire, this prospect, this thing inside me, and though I fear it will burn and mark everything it seems now too much a part of me to deny, to resist, and to feel the strength of it is to concede that it has always been present, barely acknowledged, grimly surviving in the darker parts of my ticking flesh. As I begin walking towards the gate with small, slow steps I can feel it lessening its thrashing and becoming calmer, a pure, clean feeling like the freshest of waters that lifts me as if I am the mere weight of my youth but with all the strength of my present bulk, liberty ahead of me and the chance to leave behind the foolishness of what I realise now to be a second youth, even more askew, more shameful than the milk-drenched first.

When my steps cease, when I can walk no further without touching the gate with my nose, I feel my weight falling into every hoof, settling in separate events across the small patches of ground that they cover. My head is raised and I can smell the metal in front of me, a thin scent, detected only meagrely as I am not ruled by my nostrils like a dog, but clear nonetheless and I wonder if this will be a smell that I remember, if the days and nights ahead of me are crossed in freedom, and whether coming across this smell again I will shudder, aware of the moment when I left the paddock, stepping away from it as if escaping the falling embers of what has passed before.

And though I do not know for sure if the gate is open – though I have merely responded to the sound of sliding metal that always seems to precede the opening of something – I suddenly think that perhaps this scent that licks up the damp bores of my snout is something I should avoid, I should step back from and try to blow away, it being the prelude to a mistake, hidden by a brief and hollow flaring of joy before I see that the stars above me have changed, are twisted and contorted into unrecognisable, frightening shapes, irrecoverable: the things I formed with them scattered and lost.

But this is just a flicker, an uncertainty that cannot live for long amongst the thunder growing inside me, and I am unperturbed and have not hesitated as I lower and turn my head to see the ground in one eye and the sky in the other, stretching the tip of a horn forward, feeling it glance lightly off the metal of the gate's bars before I pull back a little and feel for purchase with the point, the strange smoothness of the substance travelling down into my bones to make me shiver and flick my tail. Then I think that I have the tip pressed against its flatness and quickly I push forward, using my neck and the small step of a foreleg – and though I feel nothing I know that the horn did not slip because I felt no edge scrape against it, neither is there a beast-like shriek of metal of it opening, and so I am slow to lift my head and look ahead, uncertain of this outcome and wondering if I am not back in my stall, back amongst the strong sour scents, asleep but rapidly wakening.

But I am not displaced in that twilight. I am standing with my head raised and looking forward – looking out at the river of unobstructed land pouring out of the opened gate, the moonlight on it a suddenly incandescent mixture of blues. And the gate itself, angled back on the fence like a horse biting its own flank – I did not hear it open. Looking at it hanging limply on its post, I think that perhaps I did not hear the scrape of metal in its movement because somehow I was unaware, as if my senses at the moment of its opening were clogged with the dry mud it swung above.

I snort and swish my tail, actions like the shadows of indecision, the last commitment to my paddock before I am walking forward, my nose the first thing to pass into the new unfenced air, sucking its tingling sweetness inside me while below my hoof touches ground that seems soft and elastic in its blueness, and as I pass through the gate I find that the ground *is* different, it is not just my invention: it springs and shifts beneath the weight of my footfalls so that there is hardly any shudder to travel up my legs into my spine. And the air too is not the same – it is thicker and cooler and is filling me more easily with the slightest breath than the deepest gasp in the barn, and I raise my head higher so that the horns can slash back across the sky before throwing them down to charge forward, feeling the air whirl around my ears and down my flanks as I run with a distant rumble over the blue ground, a movement I know is not an imitation but my own device, owned solely by me and a thing begged for by this glorious moonlit night.

I stop running and come to rest, feeling that I have travelled a long distance but with no fatigue or heaving of my chest, raising my head to find that I have approached the house and am at the border where the rocky ground turns into the sharp line of grass – the beginning of the gardens which I have spent days gazing at – now just ahead of me without the links of wire to cut it into sections. The scents are strong: flowers both at the beginning and end of their lives pumping their odours into the air, while the smell of damp soil and thick leaves filled with fluid creates a wind without movement to sough against me. The grass, a mat of it lying near my hoof and running in perfect flatness to the house, has its scent too and one that wants to pull my nose down towards it, an anticipation forming of its soft bristles against my lips and in my nostrils, the freshness of its trimmed stalks a distinction from the dry and tasteless lot that is dumped in my trough, and I begin to lower my head with a mixture of habit and curiosity, the white-blue house beginning to rise out of my vision before I stop this movement, my neck pausing, the muscles there tightening so that I am frozen with my mouth above the grass.

For what do I do now? I have stepped out into freedom and yet the storm in me has vanished, it has retreated to a distant echo and I find myself unchanged: no different from feeling the hard base and corners of the trough, patiently scouring it with stretched lips for the last remnants of feed, secure in my stall or within the paddock and feeling the solidity of everything stretching from the wood around me to the stars – visible, or not but still known – above. The thought flickers through me that I might return to them, that the sky above me now I could take back into the paddock and the darkness of the barn to treasure, but even as I lift my head away from the grass I know that I will not do this, because the absence of the storm in me is just the deep suspended silence before its ferocious resumption that bursts again as I step onto the grass itself, my hooves cutting into its softness, its newness that makes the things of my past a skeleton of blackened posts, no longer a structure but its crumbling opposite.

My head is raised and I am resolved to not refill the hoof-marks in the ground behind me, and yet I find that I cannot take a step. The house is ahead of me, silent and surrounded by the gardens – the edge of which I have breached but which do not pull me forward or make me want to stay, sweet as the scents are and the soft grass beneath – and though I had always looked at this place through the fence and felt an attraction towards it, now that I find it beneath me that yearning seems misplaced. I can step towards any point that I can see – I am unhindered by wood or metal and this was the prospect that lowered my head against the gate – but amongst it, immersed in it, this freedom is another constriction, is something that makes me feel my breaths begin to tighten and my blood pump hotly into the back of my skull, a nervousness beginning to slip around my legs so that I have to skitter forward and a snort escaping my nostrils as I look around me, undecided, suddenly yearning for known channels, rutted paths that can be followed half in sleep.

A clatter and the sound of a voice comes from the house – the house that I am startled to find no more than a length from me, that I have tottered towards without awareness of anything other than my own confusion – and I stop: my sight following the smooth pale wall to the black opening that sits in it, that is not entirely dark and allures with shapes and depths that pull at my eyes. I step towards the window, whatever movement having occurred behind the wall a moment ago returning to silence so that only my hooves can be heard, creaking softly into the pliant turf – and then I hear my breaths too as I stop and raise my head, looking deeper into the house, strange and alien curves visible inside it as if looking into the ear of something.

But my interest fades and I step back from this sight, a meaninglessness eclipsing the fascination of it, and I look instead to my paddock and to the horizon of the hillock beyond it. Perhaps that is where I should go, and the instant before I am decided I feel the tightening of my breathing, as if sand is running into my lungs, a blockage caused by the frightening openness ahead of me, but one that is quickly dispersed as I move at a steady walk, the scrub suddenly hard after the grass and becoming more trodden as I near the fence. Looking at the gate bent back limply, the empty space between the posts through which I could return to the paddock a temptation, but a weak one, I slide across the wind that I imagine is trying to push me there, walking along the outside of the fence until it becomes that of the other paddock, before turning towards the horizon. I follow and turn with it as it bends away from the house, feeling the tautening and slackening of the great flesh around my shoulders and spine, a new and pleasant sensation and one that I realise is caused by movement that does not know the exact spot it will cease, that is not already carved out in the mind with the rest of me merely following. I flick my tail and feel the air as I move through it, the urge to break into a faster gait recalling the illusory lightness of youth, tempered by an emptiness, a delicate lack of need for haste because I am only heading towards the horizon, without expectation – a place I have long stared at, hazily engrossed by being able to see the beginning of the unknown beyond it.

A cloud must have drifted across the moon because the bright blue light weakens to make the stones and their shadows around me disappear. Suddenly my head feels heavy in the darkness, as if something is pushing down on it and my shoulders, and thinking that I might have encountered some fence or barrier that I cannot see, I stop – but there is nothing that I've trampled and had collapse on me, no wire or broken posts emerging as I peer into the dimness of this new terrain, and as I begin to walk again I realise that this heaviness, this feeling in my shoulders and forelegs, is only the ground rising up beneath me, the hillock beginning so that I must push my weight over something other than the flatness from barn to paddock. A few more steps and the fence has stopped to curve away again, the hill becoming steeper as I leave this line at my side, pushing me upward so that I feel a slipperiness in my stomach, the thing that I felt rising in me as I faced the open gate now so strong as I climb that I think I will totter and trip, a force pulsating up from the ground as if to serve the movement of my body, to be harnessed only by me and give me the power that if I wanted to I could slam my head into the hillside and flatten it back to level – I could spear the whole thing on my horns and rip it from the ground to reveal what is hidden beyond.

The moon emerges from its brief covering, returning to speckle the ground with the black marks and imperfections of the scrub, dispersing the dream that I might tear at the earth. The sky, choked with its shining points, is expanding as I walk so that the land is diminished, retreating beneath the black sheet that comes down on it, the line where they meet squirming in and out of my sight. I halt and turn to look behind me – I cannot see the fence and the house is now a tiny block of moon-light, its edges smeared into the land around it, and I hear none of the usual sounds that can be heard from the paddock: the rustlings of the gardens or the movement of its beasts within. This silence presses at my ears as they flick and strain, searching for something known, like the snout of a calf at the underside of its dam. And as I turn back to the nearer horizon the stars around and above me shift violently so that I am shaken by their movement, by the distance they have spun, so that I do not know how long I have stood, looking back, or been lightly plodding through this night. One or both, while not yet near to dawn, has brought me far towards it and I turn to continue up the hillock, not having heard a sound nor seen any movement from the place I have come from, now shrunk to a speck behind me.

At the horizon a filament of gold appears, a shining tendril snaking up from the earth alone before another one joins it a small distance away, each falling of my hooves beneath my gently swinging head the rhythm of their movement, that lures them further out of the ground, revealing long curving bodies of gold and white against the darkness. I think that I have seen these forms before, but never so close or low to the ground to not pain my neck. Perhaps at the end of this rise there is only more sky beneath, and I will have to turn in another direction if I do not want to fall from the land into it. I raise my head as I walk to look for the lost horizon and the border of the earth, the golden snakes growing further, and with a few more steps I must stop because suddenly I am looking down into their boiling nest: a mass of tawny stars in twisting shapes and strands all feeding into or trying to escape the same place, the lights concentrated and bright in their hues as if they have been sucked from the black emptiness. The darkness surrounding this cluster of lights I realise with disappointment to not be sky but land, the same land as that on which I am standing looking downward, and the lights as well: unfallen and embedded in the simpler firmament of earth.

I step forward, so that I can see the thing below without raising my head, one of my hooves dropping onto slightly lower ground so that I am uneven. What a strange sight, just like the things I make of the stars! But seeing the distant angular shapes nestled as tiny blocks amongst the lights I am reminded of the house and realise that man has made this, man has built this sprawling reflection of what is above, a structure already clogged with ideas and the ugliness of its imitation so that it has little attraction, can place no hooks in me to keep me rapt. And it is not silent either – sitting there beneath the moon it bleeds the tiniest of noises into the air towards me, faint echoes undetermined, and another sound like rain, or fire – a pattering noise and the crackle of shifting stones that is louder and strengthens the more I stare at its gold array, as if the sight itself causes the effect in the back of my head, an imaginary fire to consume the part of me that had not seen it.

This noise of rainfall, becoming heavier as I watch the lights below, unaccompanied by the smell of the dampening earth or the feel of thick drops across my back, makes me raise my head in doubt, and as soon as this doubt has caused the movement of my muscles to break with what I look at I know it isn't the source, it does not make the sounds that now I sense are coming from behind me. I move away from the drop in front, my hooves clacking against the stones they swipe at as I turn quickly towards the sound, a black sheet from earth to sky confronting me after the lights of below and in which I can see nothing. I step forward with head raised, testing the air for a known scent – or an unknown one – finding none except what I have moved through to get here and nothing to change the impassivity of my heart that beats no faster, that neither skips nor shimmers when the dark shape emerges from the blackness as if bursting from it, the large dog barrelling low over the ground to make the sound I heard, its thick head and small eyes fixed in my direction so that the ground between us is quietly destroyed, its thick lips and tongue a flapping canine grimace inseparable from the lust in the flicker of its eyes.

I watch blankly as the dog finishes closing the space between us, a trace of its scent reaching me along with the sound of its panting. Then suddenly it has struck at my side and I feel its weight judder through me, a shocking novelty of impact, a violence similar to the boy's thumping fist that occasionally

flashes at me as I make my way through the channel of wood, but much greater in force and the disbelief it causes: a mixture of emptiness that a growing confusion tries to fill, and pain beginning at my side where the dog has my flesh in its jaws and tugs and tries to twist its wide head, its heavy efforts pulling at me to shake my own. It growls as it does this – a jagged sound oscillating from the pleading whimper of a puppy to the low rasping growl, all of it choked with a rage I do not understand. I can only watch, neck curved, as this wildness seems to suckle from me and tries to tear me apart.

I sense a shifting of darkness in the corner of my eye, the next tug at my flank moving my head so that I see the other dog, the larger of the two, suddenly dissolving from the black, springing up from the ground to grab me. I pull my head up

– I recoil and the dog takes me at the side of the neck. I feel its teeth pressing into the flesh there and then the weight of it pulling my head back down. I am unbalanced and must take a step, and feeling this through their mouths the dogs become frenzied, their snarls and tugging movements churning around me in a storm of ferocity, while I can only stand and shudder, the pain of their assault appearing slowly in the flesh they try to tear from me.

And even though the enemy I have longed for is with me, even though its scent puts barbs in my nostrils and I am jolted and pierced, I can make no move, no swiping of horn or reordering of the ground beneath my hooves. I have left what I know and protected behind me – what is there here to protect? The dogs themselves: where previously they pulled against each other as if to split me apart, now by some alignment they seem to work together to drag me in one direction, and I am forced to stagger with their violent wrenches, my hooves scuffing against the unseen stones, my head held low and twisted by the weight clamped to my neck so that one eye is presented upward: a widened orb reflecting the stars above that are jerking and shapeless – an ugliness of light. Pain surfaces to my skin to mix with the damping blood and spit and I realise it is something I have not known – not like this, where it is being slowly forced from me – and because it is being pulled from me rather than I pulling it from myself suddenly I feel fear and danger, not the echoes of distant youth but their true forms: unfettered by ignorance, able to breathe and feed fully from everything I have witnessed and flexing through me like a whip so that I stagger from within – my body slumping down and forward onto collapsed forelegs, the dogs flushed with enough victory that their pulling lessens and they merely use their weighted jaws to hold me down, a quietness emerging, my nose pressed against the ground, the loudest thing my breaths blasting at the earth.

I do not move, I do not struggle against them because there is nothing in me! Here, held by these creatures of muscle against the land I have trespassed on I feel none of the urge, the force that would have sent me skimming across the stones of my paddock, horns lowered for a foe imagined or real. One of the dogs has started tugging again as if to turn me on my side and I lean back against its efforts, fear rising in me like a cold liquid around my lungs, the prospect of my stomach exposed to their wide jaws impelling me to try to unfold a foreleg outward – but their weight is too great and suddenly I feel a great release from my flesh: the teeth that had been lodged at my flank fall away and the black shape of the dog crosses my vision, a quick movement as it nimbly hops over my neck before I feel a new pain, a new bite and pulling at my back where both of them are now together to put me on my side. I strain against them, searching the ground beneath me with my hind legs – for its parts that aren't slippery but will try to hold me upright – but with each shaking tug that travels through me I think that if they are to pull me over, if I watch them hop and skip around my limbs to get at my stomach it will be what I should have expected at the beginning of this night when facing the open gate. I sensed the burning that would take place behind me as I left, but was blind to the punishment I would stumble into: these dogs here that try to maul me, but worse the destruction of what little spirit I had, that has abandoned me, that must have vanished like a vapour as my nose first breached the paddock's boundary.

Without anger I suddenly feel my efforts to stay upright are pointless. I do not care, because I cannot feel any link between their violence and myself and for an instant I stop fighting their heaves, as if that alone might stop them, might restore things, and this is enough that I am falling to the side where they pull, the view of askew black ground and speckled sky that my wrenched neck allows straightening as my head comes upright, my body listing and falling and my foreleg loosened from where it was compressed, unfolding so that the hoof's side is cutting into the ground – and my head, reaching the top of the arc that will end in me crashing to the earth, is high enough so that I can see back down to where I have come from, the journey I have taken on this night, my eyes galloping desperately back the way I came, towards the paddock and the house, the paddock that is not dark but blazing with a bright yellow light, all of it washed in light that makes the darkness past its hazy edge recoil and deepen.

So it burns! It burns as I thought it would! There is nothing to return to, nothing I have left behind – and then I cannot see it because I am falling, my horns and eyes tilted back by the dogs' jaws towards a different sky. But my foreleg has straight-ened further – I can feel the edge of its hoof slicing at the ground, and this blade seems to scream with its passage into the earth, as if it is a thing burning in the fire beyond and that I must stamp at to silence. And as my head is pulled back further suddenly I feel a taut and convulsing flesh at the end of my horn – not my own withers as I instantly think but one of the dogs themselves. I feel this little ball of alien flesh, my enemy, the thing that has been ripping at me, and then I feel the ground beneath my hoof and must stamp as hard as I can to silence the screaming that is not there but inside me, that has made the ground and the dog at the end of my horn a single thing, my falling weight no longer heading for the ground but pushed into the dog's side, tearing it from its hold of me as I lift it with the swoop of my neck, untangling my other foreleg so that I can skitter and then stand with the creature upraised at the end of my horn up into the darkness, a cry escaping it as it twists like a worm, a wetness forming at the top of my head.

Then its weight becomes too much and I drop my head, feeling a sudden lightness as it slips from its impalement to smack at the ground, its body rolling and the thick black ropes of its legs slapping against the scrub. The other dog has dropped from its grip of my side and so I turn to meet it. It springs to catch me again and I spin with quick footfalls so that my flank has vanished and it has jumped at nothing, and as it lands on its hind legs first with forepaws begging at the air I am at it – I have my head lowered, the points of my horns ploughing through the dirt and rocks before rising out of the earth to catch its body, and as I take its weight in my neck I feel the muscle there as if for the first time, as if it has been suddenly illuminated and I can look there: the flesh that has been the passenger to where my legs took it now their master, lifting the dog with ease on a cradle of broad head and horn before it slips out and bounces down off my flank to the ground.

I turn sharply, leaning to the side as I have seen the horse do, feeling the ground swivel and move beneath me as if it itself is the thing moved, and as I turn I am filled with a terrible thrill: an excitement that is the smell of the dogs and the night streaking into me – as solid a thing as the feel of the ground and my effortless movement over it. Then I am turned, facing the dog that is pushing itself to its feet, its wide head angled and lolling over the bulge of its shoulder so that I can see the glinting of a piglike eye. It is standing when I start running towards it, the ground snapping and crackling as hoof hits stone, a glorious heat filling my head and shoulders and fusing me to the movement I make towards the dog, which with my head raised I can see is turning to face me, the jaw falling open and lips curling back. But the sharp tooth and anger I see in it is nothing to my own and I kick harder into the ground. The dog begins a low growling and then is pacing towards me but a little out to the side – it wants to go for my neck or my flank and as we close on the other I turn my head away so that it must suddenly see a great expanse of throat, and when its paws are in the air and it is flying towards me the ground springs my shoulders up so that my hooves no longer touch it – I too am in the air but twisting so that my head is raised and then lowered, the horns that were pointing back now stabbing downward and to the side, the tip of one smashing into something hard but which instantly becomes soft. I land and try to scoop my head into this flesh, but it has already slid to the ground and I cannot tell what I trample as I turn, my hooves slipping on the dark form beneath them, the anger that was in me still pulsating with heat but lessening as my last hoof lifts from the dog and I turn again to see what might still lie there, my breaths a cadence in the darkness, the air filling me so that I am weightless, unaware of any burden in my gait.

And there, after I have turned I see on the ground the slumped shape of the dog, one leg and a part of its spine trembling, but otherwise lifeless. I can feel the blood in me as if there were another thing like eyes or ears devoted to it: it is surging through my head and around my lungs, filling my legs and the flesh at my shoulder so that I think that any creature or wall placed in front of me I could destroy – a simple charge forward with lowered head, a movement often acted out in my paddock against the heat and the air but now, here, tonight directed against the bodies of others that this impulse has craved – and I step forward hoping for life in the dog on the ground, hoping it will twist upward so that I can have the blood sing through me again and rush forward to smash it down.

But as I get closer the trembling stops and the dog becomes a corpse. I swing my head one way and then the other, looking for its partner, smelling the air and listening but I cannot see it in the varying gloom, or hear its whistling breaths, because there is another noise – one that I recognise – a low rumbling that wavers as it comes closer and I turn to face it, and when I see the shocking brightness that is suddenly before me I think that the fire has somehow spread from the house and the barn all the way to here where I stand, the same light that I saw engulfing the structures now directly on me, but heatless and without scent. I step to the side with my head raised, the blood swelling in me so that I feel the air at the tip of my horns, and suddenly the light lifts away so that I am not dazzled but can see its source: not fire but two holes making bars of white brightness attached to the thing that is lumbering roughly over the uneven ground, the rumbling from it changing tone as it pitches up and down, the beams of light lowering from the sky to touch me again like feelers.

Then I am running, down the slope towards this giant, the mass of me feeling both weightless and dangerously heavy as if all of it is at the end of my horns that are hot like limbs pulled from a fire, screaming for the cooling rush of air around them. The lights have stopped moving and the noise of it settled to a steady murmur, and with each quick and firm step towards its sudden motionlessness I watch it shrink – I see its large square shape contract and diminish until it is no larger than one of the dogs – the blood flushing through my head and around my back, another heat demanding movement as I close on it, and then I have lowered my head so that the horns point straight outward, a last kick into the ground to speed me further that lasts only a moment before I crash into it, my head and neck shuddering with the impact that I feel travel wondrously down

my spine, as if a terrible deep itch is scratched and relieved along its entire length. Then I am standing, my horns impaled, breathing deeply and seeing little before I step back, the sharp edges of metal scraping at one horn, splinters and shards of something falling around the other. Another step back and I see a single beam of dust-filled light at my side, and looking along for its source I see the vehicle I have charged, no longer dwarfed but its full and great size, many times larger than I, still murmuring and droning and from inside it looking out at me like two frightened birds the man and the boy, their eyes blank with surprise, the boy's arm raised in defence.

I stare back at them, and for a moment I am confused because I think I feel nothing – the absence of fear makes me think that I feel nothing but really my whole being is desperate, starving

for further sensation, and I launch forward again, seeing a flash of movement from the birds in their cage before my head is lowered and the vehicle is rocked on its round feet, its weight something I can feel move through me, something I can push against and have it move, its thin skin of metal closing around my horns so that I have to jerk my whole body to free them: two long scraping slides before I can raise the scorching tips into the cooler air above.

To the side there is movement and I see the man, standing with the beam of light hiding his lower half, holding something up with his arms and leaning his head over it. There is a pop like the sound of a kicked stone and I feel something land on my withers – the same kicked stone perhaps but more like the tiny bite of a blood-sucking insect – and I step back and turn towards him, excited that he is out and standing there, eager for the feel of him and what might be done to release his blood. But as I begin to trot around the end of the vehicle in his direction my limbs become suddenly heavier, as if plodding through thick and wet mud, and I slow to walking, to lower my head and smell the ground in doubt, but there is no dampness, no scent of moisture, just the dry earth, and when I try to raise my head again I find I can't – it is too heavy or too tired, or I have lost the will to do so and as soon as I think this I lose all desire for another charge, a dizzying feeling as it falls away, something as strong and solid as the ground itself no longer beneath me and I must stop, my head lowered, breathing an effort and too loud in my ears, everything around me detached and in darkness so that I may as well be asleep.

I can hear their voices, the man and the boy, but am confused as they weave around my head: noises from which ordinarily I can tell the mood of their owner suddenly without meaning or with too much, anger turning to joy and back again within a single short utterance. The distance of it – whether they are very close or far away – is a mystery as I listen, unwilling to do anything else but stare at the ground, unable to raise my head. Then I can feel one of them beside me, a movement and

slight heat at my side, an arm that I do not recognise but know
to be the boy's rising up to my withers, taking something from
there that is longer than his clasping hand, and then the other
arm is coming up and I see the rope before its loop goes over
my horns, constricting at their base, snaking down from there
over my eye that can only blink long after it has gone, the lead
pulled up and taut by the boy.

Then I am pulled. I feel the tugging at my head and know
that I will step in the direction it demands, but even though I
remember the dogs and their pulling, even though I feel a flicker
for the fight it seems like something of a different place – need-
less and merely an echo, too weak to act upon apart from the
momentary stiffening of a heel into the ground. There is a dull
thudding on my rump and I try to angle my head to see what
it is as I am led, but suddenly the ground is sloping upward
and feels different. I sense the vehicle, large and open in front
of me – the thudding increases at my rear and my head is
tugged violently, the rope a straight line disappearing into the
black space of the vehicle's insides. I step away from the thudding and find that I am going up the slope, that the rope is
pulling me up the ramp that is soft and bending beneath my
weight, the sound of my hooves on the metal distant, and then

suddenly a loud and frightening clatter – and then I am in the vehicle, my head still held taught by the rope, my fear lessening to be replaced with blankness. The only thing I feel a dull perception of heat, perhaps gained in the day, leaching out of the metal towards me.

I move forward and the rope slackens and I turn my head, looking with one eye to the square of night behind me, the stars visible in a strip of sky, meaningless and sparking no interest in me, while below I see the man and the boy, their torsos and heads emerging from the vagueness of the ground. The man is holding something – the same thing he held to his shoulder and that he must have used to beat at my rear, but now it is bent and draped across his arms while the boy, he too is burdened and is struggling to drag something into the vehicle, a large shape the man must help him with and that flops loudly onto the metal ramp, and that I realise to be one of the dogs. I shuffle forward and feel a wall come up against the side of my head but am able to angle it further within the slack of the rope, can watch with nearly both eyes as the boy disappears and then returns either instantly or after a while with the second dog – again the struggle as both he and the man lift it onto the ramp and drag it up into the vehicle. When they finish they both slowly stand and turn to me: I see their eyes pass over me briefly and then they turn and begin along the ramp, hopping down to disappear at either side. A scraping noise and the ramp is coming up, the opening beginning to contract as if a mouth is gulping up the ground and the strip of sky above it, to leave me and the two corpses in darkness.

But before the rumbling begins again in front of me, before the vehicle starts to move and I am jostled and must struggle to keep my balance, I hear a quiet whistling rhythm, a sound I know but that I struggle to identify, my thoughts scratching around like birds in the dust until I realise it is one of the dogs still breathing. I hear its last breaths – pained and lessening into nothing and with these sounds it comes back to me, the relish of earlier sensation, as real and strong a memory as if I were still amongst it and I feel excitement flowing through my legs and shoulders and into the rope to make it taut, each receding gasp of the hound a reminder of what I did to it, what I have created in its destruction, and I close my eyes to better feel the blood wash around me – the blood I know I share with others.

CHAPTER 6

The Grey is opposite, his head hidden but a small patch of his rump and swishing tail visible as the sound he makes repeats itself in the warm air of the barn: a clanking of metal, a noise softened by the darkness formed in contrast with the great, bright sunlight coming through the open door, and thinly shafting down from the holes in the roof above us. My body rests on the floor of my stall, which is damp and filled with scent but cooler than the air above it, a coolness that my flesh is pushed into and splayed wide by its own weight, my eyes closing as I lie here and opened by the buzzing of an insect, the flick of an ear. It is the hottest part of the day and the stifling suns that pass feel as if they have always been and will never end – the middle of summer – the hazes that rise from the ground seeming to fill everything that must breathe and I most of all to leave me drowsy, uninterested in the tongues that drink from my eye, or the stench in which I am lying.

I am not asleep and will not sleep, but I am quiet as I watch what little of the horse I can see in front of me, and I do not flinch at the noise he makes – nor am I repelled by the urine that I can feel both on my stomach and in my nose because all my senses are pointed inward. The flies lick at the veined bases of my eyes because I am looking back to the night, between now and which many days have passed in quiet heat – time spent neglecting the stars and the growths in the paddock, hoping for moments like this in the barn where if I am careful and still I can let my mind slip into memory, the thoughts of that night sending flickers of excitement and sensation out into my body, shimmers that seem to weaken and then might explode in me with such force that I think I am running and can feel the mauled flesh at my flank, the shudder of my back as my horn punctures the dog's ribs to part its insides.

And though these recollections spring from my flesh and not my eyes, distanced as I am to what happened by the days that have elapsed, I fear they might be illusory: perhaps they are merely something else I have built – like the shapes I think I see in the stars, unreal and slowly fading – and soon I will be left with nothing but ungraspable traces, useless itches in my mind and spine that nothing can reach or alleviate. I rise and plod heavily over to my trough, feeling a jagged confusion of hunger and thirst, not for the food or the dirty remnants of water that my breath ripples as I lower my head, but for something that is too vague until I turn and begin walking away from the trough, then suddenly in the movement I remember it – the surge in my chest and the heat at my horns as I faced the dog before charging, the spinning of that impulse as it welled in me before snapping taut to send me forward, full of a strength I did not know existed, had only suspected might be there and that was suddenly mine to possess, to point the force of horns and spine in the direction that I chose.

More dreams to haunt me in this humid box of the barn? It is there and not there, memory and feeling weaving up into my mind before disappearing to echo in my flesh – an elusiveness to which I have become attached like a nail in wood – wanting desperately to feel again as I did then even if it is a deception, and only in the misted form of memory.

Now there is a slight noise and the light coming through the open door is altered, something I do not see directly but can feel as if it were a solid thing touching me. I turn from the trough and move along the stall's fence to look through an opening and there in the doorway is a strange sight: a bright golden orb above a patch of bright blood red. It moves forward and a small figure appears – a small boy, his torso and arms red and the hair of his head so flaxen that it is almost white, two thin brown twigs for legs poking into the ground like stakes. I press forward against the fence, the wood sharp at my snout and creaking loudly enough to make the boy twitch and his legs compress – I can see him looking for the source of the sound and then he must see me – I watch the slight wince that he makes when he is peering in my direction and then he turns and gestures to the side and another child appears: a girl, again awash in bright red and with the same thin spokes holding her up, the same light yellow hair, but wild and curling around her head so that standing there she blazes with light and I am startled, the fence creaking loudly so that they both jump as if bitten or stung, the girl's arm reaching out for the boy, she much bigger than him yet still small herself.

With the arm that touches him she pushes, and the boy jerks forward towards me, turning and hissing back at her. For a moment they look at each other, and I can see their profiles, silhouetted against the brightness of the afternoon, so similar that they must share the same blood, the same little stub of nose and chin reflecting each other, and now the boy is stepping slowly into the barn, edging his way in while staying as far as possible from my eyes and gaping nostrils that watch and suck at him through the gaps of wood. The girl follows, beginning slowly and then rushing towards the boy until they are touching, their backs pressed against the wall near the doorway, the boy crammed into the corner where the opposite row of stalls meets the wall. I cannot see the horse and he has stopped his clanking, so he must also sense them, even though they are very quiet and in the gloom away from the entrance. Then the girl steps away from the boy and directly towards me, reaching out with one foot before joining it with the other, creeping closer this way while the boy hisses a mixture of fear and encouragement behind her until she is close enough that a few more steps would have her at my stall.

The boy is edging up to join her, using her to block his sight of what he nears and I watch quietly, smelling the unfamiliar scents that reach me, looking to the girl's eyes that have shown nothing but fear and a mocking excitement, that do not seem to see me except as something fearful, and it is only after I have remained still and she has mirrored this stillness with her brother clutching her arm that her raw excitement subsides and I can see what she sees: the massive dark head obscured and caged by the wooden frame it tries to push through, the white of an eye prominent in the blackness, the horns hidden except for their tips that break the line at the top of my stall and all of it impossibly large, as if I am the size of the barn itself – a size that swells further when I look to the boy's more frightened eyes.

And looking at them in turn, shifting my head against the fence, I watch how they disfigure me: the boy, fascinated by my eye, makes it swollen to the size of his head, a mass of black and white rolling in its oil, revolting him every time it passes as if he will be slimed by it, while the girl – for her it is the bulk of my body, the shoulders and neck around the head inflated so that my head is dwarfed, a tiny stump comprised of two gaping nostrils stuck to the expanse of mass, of heavy muscle and fat that sits behind it. Perhaps this is how I am truly formed, grotesque and imbalanced, and the other images I have seen are my own construction. But as I shift in the stall with the sudden fear of this, the concentration of the two before me is broken – they cower and grasp at each other with small hands as I step back to turn my head, to thrust it forward into the space in the fencing and see them differently, to see what they see differently, their eyes darting over me and the thin structure that separates us before they return to mine and I can see myself, huge and restored, a shifting blackness in the dim stall.

They fear me but what are they afraid of? Nervousness makes them still, as if they have prodded something they think is a hive, awaiting the outcome. I snort and they flinch; I push harder against the wood of the fence, hard enough to make it move and squeal and they step back together, squealing themselves, afraid but with the eagerness and spirit of young dogs. And now the boy is pulling at the red that covers him, is lifting it over his head so that he can hold it in his hands towards me, a bright scarlet thing rippling in the sunlight washing through the doorway. I lift my head and strain to smell what it is he holds. There is no smell that is new for this object, but the boy himself seems encouraged and takes a step forward, leaving the grip of his sibling, holding the garment in front of his waist so that his abdomen is obscured and jerking it towards me so that it flashes red and shadow in the light, flapping quietly like a wing.

I look from the twitching cloth to his face, nearer and clearer than it has been before, and suddenly in his eyes the playful fear recedes and is replaced by something else – the same aversion I have seen in those that tend me, or look down at me from above the horse. And that repulsion, that disgust that I see most strongly in the man – is it the twisted growth of youth, coming from when everything was larger, more deformed and frightening? Or is this boy already pinning his anger and frustration to my side, things that I can see flickering in his tiny body before me, even now in his early youth before its violence has truly risen, thinking that he shakes and taunts me with a rag the colour of blood but unaware that what he really does is see more than just a darkened shape of eyes and horns and massive flesh, but the traces of things that will slither up his bones and into his growing flesh.

The boy emits a short high mocking sound and then turns back to his sister, his small back a patch of light flesh, ribs visible beneath the skin as the dogs' ribs were when their heads were stretched to the side. The girl seems intent to leave – she has taken a step towards the bright doorway – but the boy points to the opposite stalls and calls to her. She follows his arm and eyes as do I, shifting slightly against the fence, and there is the Grey, his head above the fence, ears pricked and nostrils dilating curiously with each intake of air he tries to inhale from around the watching pair. He stands motionless and swishes his tail, a soft recurring sound like a breeze or the breath of a parent, and suddenly the boy and girl are walking towards him, the girl cooing and taking the lead, the boy covering his torso again in red and following her, the fear they had for me lifted from the movement of their limbs and the carriage of their heads, that now bend towards the Grey like flowers on thin stalks. They are close enough to the fence that the horse can stretch over and touch them with his nose, the girl pushing forward her stomach so that it bumps the grey muzzle, and she does not recoil when the lips reach out and take the red fabric away from her skin, her hand coming up to stroke the front of the head that tugs and pushes at her gently. The boy moves close and when he raises his arm the Grey flinches a little but accepts his hand, a small pale object like the foot of a bird patting at his neck.

I watch and wait for the slight compression of that long neck that will send the teeth out at them, but it does not come: the horse stands and is petted and rubbed, his tail still swishing and his head nudging their hands and arms upward, but that is the only movement, the only expression he chooses. Then the boy is crouched on the floor, the disappearance of his legs making him a tiny red and flaxen shape, his hands scrabbling at the floor like a chicken, collecting a few broken and dirty stalks from the ground that he offers to the Grey, standing before him with his hand upraised, the snout with its deep nostrils finding the hand and weighing heavily in it, and seeing this I feel a horrible slithering inside me, as if my flesh is being wrung like something wet, because I suddenly remember what it feels like to have a small hand at the end of my snout, a hand cupping milk that my long tongue wrapped around and pressed against, sometimes leaning into it for the support my own legs still had not mastered, the child before me and that I wanted to lean against but couldn't for the thin wood slats of the stall, dipping its hand in the bucket to bring it back up to my mouth, warm milk running down its arm, streaked with a little red from a cut on my tongue, a tongue that had explored every part of the stall – the wood and all its edges – for something ungraspable. I can taste the sickly mix of milk and iron now as I stand here, and the texture of the child's hand, the owner of which I wanted to feel, to have its warmth pressed against my side.

The shame of youth!

Was it there that I was begun, that I became the creature of stall and paddock? And that stall itself, the one where I was suckled from an unknown child's hand, a figure I would never see again – the same place where the man held the girl above me and where she would come to sit by me alone – how thin that wood was!

If it were here now it would not hold the turning of my head – I could have broken from it in that youth and yet chose not to, was content to scour my trough and sleep as if preparing for the long nights spent looking upward, the flesh burning at my neck.

These children in front of me, these carriers of perfection in everything but proportion, their skin and hair and even their movement unweathered, untouched by anything, all of it protected by youth, a disgusting thing, more repellent than the urine beneath my hooves, and I can feel my flesh tightening, the slackness pulled taut by the thick lengths of sinew and a heat beginning to pulse along my spine. The breaths I take sink deeper – I feel the air travelling inward and the heat beginning to burn at my back, and suddenly it is the small figures before me that are the cause of it, that are the fuel for the thing that is making me breathe and choke at the same time. I feel great warmth in my body but an ice behind my eyes and I push against the fencing to make their small bodies turn, their faces curious at the noise and then turning to surprise as I begin to clamber at the fence and the trough attached to it, wildly kicking my hoof out, pawing with it like a dog might until I have raised it high enough that it is in the trough and I can pull myself upward, raising my head above the fence to look down at the children, two puny vessels of blood and bone looking up to me with horrified faces, an enormous head of unnatural breadth reflected in their eyes, the horns raised like the wings of a raptor and still beneath it the body beginning to breach the fencing, so large to them that its end is lost in darkness.

I snort and they cower, their backs bending and the boy's hands darting outwards, the girl's clutching hers at her stomach. The trough beneath me is moving slightly, it and the fence it is attached to swaying forward as I push with my hind legs and kick blindly with a foreleg and swing my head from side to side, the burning of my back now in the tips of my horns and making me want only to scramble over this structure that hinders so that I can cool them in the youth before me, to lift and break these vessels and feel the sickness leak from them, to know again the size and strength of my body: the power I have to create new things from the impact and fusion of myself to the delicate frames of others. Again I flail a hoof at the fence above the trough but I cannot climb any further – I am frustrated – the children are moving cautiously towards the door, holding on to each other, and I cannot get at them, but even this is a wonder, is a pleasure, to feel a desperate want denied, and I marvel at its strength – this thing within me, that makes me stand where I would normally eat and only seem to know of a single thing, little aware of much else.

Together the children slip out through the doorway, disappearing into the sunlight in flashes of red and gold, small scraping noises replaced with silence and then a snort from the Grey, and the creaking of wood that suffers beneath my weight. The light that is in the barn, the wide swathe coming through the door and the thin bars from the roof swing across the ground as I stand and breathe, hanging on to dissipating sensations, beginning to feel the movement of the wood as it faintly sways, in rhythm with my lungs. Then I push back from the trough and climb down into my stall, not knowing how long I have stood there with my head raised in the air, set still by the desire to get at what was before me, but also frozen by the things that emerged for me to see without my eyes as if for the first time, as if emerging from darkness – things disjointed and disturbing until suddenly I realise they are not separate but one thing, they belong to one thing and when I turn and move into the stall there is a shadow that does the same. A shadow not sprung from my hooves and flattened on the ground but made from the glare of these things that I am beginning to see, and when

I turn my head to look at the fence of the stall, a weak section with bits of wood attached chaotically to others, this other bull turns also, and we both look at this barrier and feel the strength within us, the power and weight that our hooves only need send forward.

I step towards this fencing, the ribs of weak wood attached to a breakable spine, bringing it closer to my lowered head, when I am stopped by a noise to the side – the familiar scraping of the doorway over the earth and the light of the afternoon bursting through where a moment ago was blackness. I have stopped and my head is turned towards the square opening, the sky a deep blue above the ground, the sides of the channel of wood visible and disappearing towards my paddock. And seeing this I feel a poison within me, a surging of something akin to pain, a shudder of fear that beats at my lungs and averts my head – because suddenly there is no desire for the stall's fence on my horns; I do not want to feel the burning above my head or the levering of bone from muscle, and all the memories, the sensations of anger and wild freedom, the rising of which I welcomed, are as empty as smoke, as useless as the mist at dawn, and they drop away from me heavily to leave me staggering with the new weight of their absence. I step towards the opening,

trotting towards the light and out onto the rutted pathway, aware of the wood at my side, its solidity banging and scraping against my flanks, but more aware of the terrible neglect I have given to the things I valued, the things in my paddock and the sky above, and I am almost running between the two fences, dust and a pattering kicked up by my hooves, fear and a hotness suppressing my breaths until I am into the paddock and breathing heavily, an alien place, changed and overgrown without my consent, all that I have built lost within the passing shadow of sensation and the blinding hunger for it.

A bird lands ahead of me within the tangle of weeds, and, looking at it, watching its small form twitching and revolving its tiny head, suddenly I am horrified because I realise what it is – a little bitter fruit of suffering that has precipitated from

the air. It looks around not with an eye searching for the next fencepost or branch to discover and rest, but the next safe place where it will not be leapt at by a cat, or swooped down upon by another bird. How I have envied them, these birds and even the creatures on the ground: they who can decide to leap away and with a flick of freedom be somewhere else, be unconfined. And yet they are even more enclosed than I am, because while they eat what they want and move where they want and have the appearance of domain within the wild, they are in fact ruled, caged by nature, by fear of danger, of starvation and death. What is freedom for them but fear and more fear?

There is part of me that wants to charge at this bird, to run it down and make it leap and flap its way somewhere else, but the feeling is weak and I turn from it. The sun is low in the sky and I watch it and listen to the rustling the bird makes with its investigation at my side, my eyes dropping to the ground around me, watching the shadows lengthen on the thin stalks, the shadow bull that was with me not long ago now remote, weakened and exhausted, trapped between my heart and lungs as if it were a stone.

CHAPTER 7

A different night and I am back in the barn. I was sleeping but now am awake, the sound of something half in memory and half unknown, the thing that opened my eyes to see nothing but the darkness around me, familiar shapes and structures sprouting from it with each blink, but slowly so that I feel I cannot move. Then there is the sound again to fill the part of my memory that had lost it, coming from the wall, and like the sliding of a bolt but not where it should be, at the other end from where the opening is that leads me to my paddock and so I turn my head to face this curiosity, this difference to the night itself, with a dull expectancy, wondering whether I already betray the previous days and nights of perfect observation by the flashing hope – sparked by this sound and already vanished – that they will be destroyed.

In the patterned darkness that my head points to there is silence, made deeper by my probing sight, that is becoming filled with more shapes and textures except that I can see what looks like a patch of sky – a small dog's leg worth of stars and their surrounding black depth – and I think that perhaps the noise I heard was a part of the barn falling to the earth, a sloughing of one of its wooden scales to give me a fissure to the night outside, an opening against which I can press my eye and ear, and continue to consume, long after my trough is empty. And the flashing desire I had for destruction, for the abandonment of inaction and return to the lust of memory: it lived fleetingly and now I have this window to the sky, as if to mock me, as if it were the thing that has beaten those desires away, and I only notice them in their passing.

And then I smell the freshness of the air, pouring through this gap to disperse a bit of the stench around me, pulling me forward to take a step into its flow, my eyes beginning to see everything clearly from beneath a final blink, watching as the patch of stars grows to become not a mere hole, but a gap in the wall of the barn that stretches down to the ground. Then there is a sound that makes me jolt my head: the familiar sound of wood scraping over stones, the gap becoming larger to reveal more sky and some open ground beyond it and I realise that I face a door – another doorway to leave the barn, not yet large enough that I could get through it, but expanding in stutters as if something is pulling at it.

There is a movement on the door, at the side of it, along the edge that cuts into the sky and the ground beyond. I feel a ripple through my head and neck to see the long legs of a spider reaching around to climb onto the inward side, to perhaps then scurry into the barn, except that it pauses and raises a huge abdomen, a tapered silhouette that grows impossibly large until I realise that the entire edge of the door has shifted, is a moving black mass that is not a spider or its horde but the girl of the house following the crawling progress of her hands, carefully stepping around into the opening so that she can press herself on the wood and lean against it, jolting her weight forward to travel down her thin arms, achieving a scrape of wood against stone with each effort. She continues pushing, and I am frozen as I watch her, the sky and earth expanding, no longer slivers but large patches, swathes of space that I might walk out into, and I feel the turning of something very small deep within my chest as if something is being gathered – but then the door opens abruptly and the girl loses her balance and falls quietly to the ground, climbing up from her knees and brushing at herself with her hands, turning and disappearing out of sight while I remain standing, deep within the barn, seeing the framed openness that spins my breath and heartbeat around the other.

I move slowly within my stall, the smell of night stronger with each step, a sweet and clear freshness that demands to be split apart so that I trot forward and out into it, the sky above my head domed and speckled, the ground beneath me hard muddied sand overgrown with tall weeds – while in a curve that grows out from the barn behind there is a solid fence, a wall that runs in a wide arc to encircle me and touch the barn again, the same long curve I have seen from my paddock, yet now I stand inside it. Is this to be my new paddock? I turn to look back and see that the door to the barn is still open, a rope snaking down from it and running towards where the curved wall begins its growth from the barn before ending in a large coil on the sand. Perhaps I am now to have the run of my stall and this enclosure, never to see the white and bright colour of the house, or look over at the horse in his own paddock. Because the walls of this one are too high – they are high enough that only sky is visible at their top edge from where I stand, as if the ground beneath me has sunk, has been pushed down by the sudden event of my weight.

I walk forward and feel the cling of growths at my legs.

Nothing has stood or moved over this ground for a long time – the things that are growing here are elongated and weak, they have not been strengthened by the scythe or stamp of a mislaid hoof, and while they wrap themselves around the black limbs that rustle them they are a weak net, easily pierced. If I am to live here I will change that, I will crush all of these growths so that anything that then pokes from the ground will not be from a paddock that did not have me in it. And I am beginning to feel a cold excitement, deep and evenly spread as if it is in every part of me quietly rather than a screaming in my head and horns: the prospect of this paddock and the opportunity to begin again, new things to watch or crush and have possession of, a beginning at the point of which no error can possibly be made or deficiency felt, no hunger for sensation that I sense now is dying in me, killed like a trodden snake by this greater prospect spread around me and safely enclosed.

But there is something else in this paddock, here with me as I begin to trample around the flat area I have made in the weeds, turning in a circle until I look back to the open door and the rope leading away from it, coiled in a heap by the wall and the plants trying to scrabble onto it, as if their leaves are limbs that will give them leverage – and then I realise what it is within these walls with me – another bull, my smaller weaker youth, bursting from the same opening and out into bright daylight, hearing something to my side and turning before charging at the figure who held the rope in his hands that had opened the door, the ground uncluttered with any growths and passing quickly under me a flash of yellow as I ran with my head held high, a head not yet weighed down by the flesh I carry now, the figure scrabbling over the wall but still holding the rope so that it rises from the ground, a sound coming from him and from many others like him visible around the top of the wall: men clustered like birds, enjoying the scene beneath. I have been in this paddock before, was sometimes let into it in my youth to scurry about after men that would themselves scurry over the walls like cats, the impulse to run at them half-formed but eager, my head held up and awkwardly with only a final, tentative swipe of my horns, even though they were out of reach.

Away from memory I look to the high edge of the wall, searching for the round forms of their heads, thinking that this is not where I will reside but instead am brought here to retread those paths and re-enact the shame of that mockery. Except that it will be different now – and this makes me snort and shake my head – because I know what it is to feel the power of my body strike through that of another, what it is like to have the ground turn beneath you at your will, to suck them towards my lowered horns rather than scratch over dust and sand to get at them. There are no heads, no figures at the wall, but it does not stop the feeling, the rage, from pumping out from my heart into my flesh, the thing that I thought was dead or an illusion alive and thrashing within so that I have to stamp and turn one way and the other, hoping for them, willing them to be present somewhere in the paddock with their shifting coloured sheets out-held as they did then, not caring for anything but this desire, the prospect of the paddock itself meaningless and then absent, filled and blocked out by the sudden certainty streaking through my blood.

And through the tangled mess of vegetation I see a figure, the rounded shape of a head in the dimness, bobbing above the stalks and moving in an unknown direction – perhaps away or towards me, the head glistening in what little light there is from the stars and sliver of moon above – and I recognise the great mass of hair on her head and see it bunching over her shoulders: the top part of the girl, stepping through the weeds and towards the clearing I have made. A spasm in my shoulder and

I am stamping at the ground, a prickling heat smearing my neck and the back of my head, my eyes feeling as if they are burning as I watch her part the last of the thin and dying stems, placing a foot through first into the clearing and onto the soft hay-like substrate before the rest of her slips out with a flicking twist of her body and she is before me. I wait for the taunting, for her arms to snap out as if holding something, the heat boiling in me and searing in my horns and at my hind, the impulse in me to run at her twisted around the things in my chest, a tight and wondrous knot of feeling that I hold and cling to, both wanting and forbidding its release, waiting for the stamp of foot or flicker of hand that will send me forward.

But the last of her slips through the weeds to become a clearer shape in front of me, one of her hands the last thing to appear, snaking out to join her body at her side and as it does so, suddenly she changes: she is no longer a thing behind the wooden bars of stall or fence but a presence that is unobscured, unprotected by my own encirclement, her form not seen in segments through slats in wood but complete and more powerful, a strength visible in her flesh where before was merely spindle – and seeing this I am shocked so that it feels as if the air is blocked and I must stop at the top of my breath – because there is no fear in her as there has been in all the others that have been this close to me, those that would challenge and goad me. She stands without threat or posture, her body moving slightly with her own breaths, each intake making her larger before me, filling her shoulders to move the hair on them in a faint and listless wing-beat.

Then she turns her back to me and I stagger forward, the impulse to charge her snapping inside me but unconnected to my legs, still the total lack of fear or nervousness in her the barrier, the thing that means I only lurch a few steps with my head raised. She is making her way down the thin path she has herself trampled through the weeds, and I watch her, the dark head with its mass of hair and the body beneath it receding down this channel, the sides of which are made more solid by the night, making me think that they would press against me if I followed her. She diminishes further, and when she disappears it is the fear that she will escape that pushes me through the undergrowth after her, rustling through it in a quick trot, expecting to find her facing me and stamping the ground, shouting and goading, a provocation she may have survived to slip over the wall when this ring was open sand, yet one she will not now.

But suddenly I have burst through the weeds, my hooves are on soft sand alone and I am in an open space, the ground in front unpopulated by any growths, the wall visible ahead as it curves around, a part of it jutting out sharply into the ring – the girl standing by this part, this opening beyond which I can see the land spilling away into the gloom of night and distance, unfenced. Then the girl turns to me and raises her arm: she performs the same beckoning movement I have often seen and ambled towards, the pale arm arcing out and then to her chest – but whereas before I have felt my neck itch with the eagerness for her fingers, now that she stands before me with no wood or metal between us this movement turns something within me, it twists me as if I am watching the stars above, for what is this power compared to mine? What is this gesture from a small creature that I have been beckoned by, hoping for short relief from the numbness in my withers, not knowing that I could have at any time gouged her through the fencing as she pressed against it to reach me, that such an event would have given me more than her idle fondness ever did?

And a gate is open: this part of the wall which angles into the ring leaves a wide space beside her, large enough that I could easily walk through. There is none of the hesitation in me, the stuttering of feeling I had when before I faced freedom, and which led me over to the house and into its gardens – yet I do not bolt for the openness ahead, I do not skim my hooves over this soft sand and past the girl because she is there, standing with little movement, a possibility as rich as that of freedom: the chance to destroy what is before me, to crash against the things that surround me always and fill my eyes and ears, blocking them, stopping me from sensing what it is that my amassed flesh and point of horn demand. I raise my head to look at her better, feeling the weight of it all on the thickness of my neck, her small but forceful frame with the hand curving towards me again not the thing that makes my leg move; a single step and then another so that I am walking slowly in her direction, my head held high so that my eyes are on her, my breathing calm as even now I try not to feed what it is in me that wants to destroy everything that I have known – these quiet intakes a last resistance to the thing that is rising in me, the desire to burst forward with head lowered suddenly becoming fused to my will to make it richer and more powerful than anything before, a vast sky of sensation so that I am both sinking and ascendant.

From walking I accelerate, still trotting with my head up

before I feel a looseness in my neck that begins to drop my horns, the air becoming noticeable against me and in my ears, each movement of shin and haunch an easiness and a pleasure because now I am not forced by the attack of another – I am not made to defend myself against tooth and jaw with a desperate clutching of the stronger parts within me, now I have them collected in my chest: I choose to push myself forward with the intent to shatter what it is before me, and as the sight of the girl enters me before I drop my head fully I feel a perfect rhythm from the night, a pulse from everything around me, from the ground beneath to the girl ahead drawing closer, the voices I can suddenly hear syncopating from around the top of the wall not a shock but a part of it too, their rage and excitement pushing me faster as their screams echo around the ring.

I look to the girl's head and her own excitement, the triumph in her raised chin and nose and the curve of hand towards the open gateway, gesturing. But as the sound of rumbling hooves rises to her ears and I am almost upon her, she realises that the line I take is not for the exit but for her. Then my head is down and I cannot see her – she has become a slight impact and a lightness on my neck, all the force and strength that was visible in her when unobstructed an illusion as I lift her and she flops onto my shoulders. For a moment her legs falling down each of my flanks so that I carry her, to the shrieking encouragement of those that must watch, their heads hiding in the dark – and I carry her until I must turn to avoid the wall of the ring and she slips off and falls to the ground, the sound of it a light thump between my hoof-falls, that lessen like the rushing air as I stop.

I turn quickly, flushed with feeling and happiness, curious to see what I have done, what remains on the ground and whether it will need beating down again. I take eager steps forward and then stop, because there is a known voice to my side and I turn my head to see the boy of the farm, shouting at me, waving his arms, coming towards me as he always has with his own eager brutality. He shouts again and in that instant I run for him, his body terribly small and naked with no fence between us, a useless thing that has wielded sticks and blows against my disinterested flesh, but a flesh that is now keen in everything it does and this most of all: the unfettered impulse forward, the rush of air and rumble of hooves bringing me to his little figure that turns and begins running for the wall, and I think that I will raise him up and pin him against it – except that suddenly the wall is in front of me and only his foot remains before slipping over its top edge.

My weight still pushes me forward though my hooves have stopped and I hit the wall, my neck bending as I try to get the horns away from it. The boy has escaped but the girl must still be there and so I turn, feeling the ground revolving and spinning everything around me until the heap of the girl is before me, is in the line from my hooves to my tail and then I begin slowly along it, looking to the heap that grows and shifts so that she must be trying to get up, a dim shape that will climb up to face a much darker one – and I can smell blood coming from her and other smells as I continue walking, feeling everything of the ground and the air and the sky above passing in and out of me as if I am a part of them and they are a part of me, watching as the heap rises into one form and then another, far bigger than just the girl alone and I start to trot at this new and welcome enemy, wondering at its mass and texture, the boy's voice chasing me and trying to turn me, I know, but this thing ahead more interesting: the girl is amongst it at its highest point and then I realise she is held by the man and a woman. They are running awkwardly for the opening, burdened with her limp body, and I charge after them, relieved of all that has gone before, heavy and fast and bringing them nearer to me, a length away from their many disordered legs that slip through the opening, the girl dropped in the woman's arms as the man turns and begins to close the gate on my approach, the opening diminishing until I am diverting to a section and then a mere crack in the wall before it cracks shut and I stop, sand and stones kicked up from my hooves the only thing to crash into it.

I turn and step back to look at the wall, to face the part that was open, but which now joins seamlessly to the rest of the curve that runs away on both sides to encircle me. At the top of this wall a head has appeared – the man – his face turning away to look down at something I cannot see and then back at me, and even in the dim light I can distinguish the anger in the muscles above his eyes, the curl of lips to show a glint of teeth. A high wailing voice emanates towards me from the wall: what must be the woman crouched behind it, her screams rising into the sound of something desperate and then suddenly softening, the man turning to look down again and disappearing, his own voice seeping through the wall, low and thickened with anger and then changing to join hers in a higher, more peaceful tone. To the side there is a noise and a slight turn of my neck makes me see the boy's head, moving quickly along the top of the curve as if flying, shouting with a deep fear in his voice that does nothing to interrupt the soft tones of the man and the woman, who only reply when he calls again more urgently and loudly, their voices in unison, light with the passing of danger.

The boy disappears too and I remain standing, looking at the blank and tightly knit wood in front of me, feeling my unhurried breath being pulled deep into my lungs, the heat and lightness of my flesh only beginning to rest, to become again a burden. The man's head appears and I jerk my head upward to this orb poking above the wall, quickly joined by the boy's, two sets of eyes looking down at me and with such hate and anger that I cannot see myself, I cannot see what they see but only what they feel, the richness of which I drink and enjoy as if from the freshest of rainwater, pushing it down into me so that I will have it always: their rage, their abhorrence for the bull, their fear and disgust that makes me feel as if I am falling away from them, a strange and compulsive tightening at the back of my neck raising my head and horns into it, pulling me up so that they are diminished before me.

But I am drawn back towards them when I realise that they are struggling. It feels as if I swoop birdlike from where I have been down to their heads above the wall, these orbs moving and jerking, facing the other at angles that shift and turn as they seek dominance over the other, their fighting bodies hidden, the man growling at the silent boy before jerking back and away from him and holding something up in the air – the same long and glinting thing I have seen before – and I wonder if it was that which brought me down, though I did not hear it's shot. The boy is still fighting with the man, but only with his voice, while the man looks to me and lowers his arm and for a moment his hate recedes enough that I see myself flicker across his face – a brief release before his anger returns to cloud me – but clear enough that I see he will not strike at me, he will not try to kill me as both he and the boy crave, because I see in him that somehow I am the trough to which they lower their heads, the stone above my neck and shoulders the same stone of the thick walls which protect them, the thought of destroying me enough to frighten the man so that he can only stand without moving.

And seeing this it is as if all the wood around me has suddenly turned to dust, has crumbled and will disappear from the merest snort of my lowered breath. I stand and stare at the man, knowing he is afraid, willing him to clamber over the fence and into the ring, watching his anger diminish so that I must turn to the boy to find a glimmer of its former richness. Then I begin to step and turn away from them, the barn entering my vision from the side as I swing my head around, the open door visible as a patch of blackness in the dark blue gloom. But I do not head towards it. I am content to stand, breathing quietly, nursing all the memory in my head and muscle to suckle the thing inside me: the growing shadow of myself that now I see clearly. And I stand like this until I notice that the sky has turned grey, and is lightening.

CHAPTER 8

Everything is a hotness and my mouth is dry, my tongue sitting in it fat and cracked as if I have eaten the earth beneath. Ahead is the doorway unchanged, a distant opening visible over the weeds and growths in the large wall of the barn, the smell of the horse and stronger that of water occasionally leaking from it to where I still stand, to turn my head and almost force a step in its direction. But still I do not move, I have not moved since turning from them: their heads resting on the wall drained of feeling, exhausted from the contortions of hate and anger I put in them – and without those creations of little interest. Even when the stars appeared again above me I did not step or lift my head, their shimmering and movement weak compared to that which I have watched inside me, have felt burgeoning within until I do not need the eyes of others to see myself, but can merely close my own to see the bull standing there, the muscle and power no longer hanging on its bones to push it to the ground but lifted, suspended like a black liquid to ripple between the ground and sky.

Again the scent of water, sharp and bright, enters my nose. I breathe it in and feel the distant but nearing urge to drink, that I must drink – and yet I fear that to move now will be to destroy everything I have within me: a solitary step and the bull I can see will vanish to become again just the hard little seed between my heart and lungs, and that the walk to the barn will be a heavy one, mired in loss.

But when the scratching and throbbing of thirst has blossomed in every part of me, the closing of my eyes only forming the dancing of fire-like lights, then I step forward across the sand, a movement tottering and irregular with the stiffness that has suddenly formed in my legs and back, a thing I had been blind to while standing, and has already disappeared when I begin splitting through the growths, the aperture black and growing ahead, breathing on me the scents of its insides, attractive and repellent, pulling my eager nose. Then the barn is large enough before me that I cannot see the sky above, the opening more solid than its wood surrounds and I lower my head to puncture it, sudden darkness cutting everything from my eyes and ears so that I trot and stumble to the trough, my tongue resisting and then accepting the liquid there as I drink, the rasping noise of the metal around my head joined by another: a pattering coming from outside the barn and a loud bang that jolts my head upward and away from the water with nose dripping, a minor turn of my neck to look behind and I see that the door to the ring has been closed. I hear a scraping of metal, what must be the sound of old and stubborn bolts being forced across, a slower pattering that recedes and vanishes and then I am alone in the half-darkness.

I lower my head and drink again until my tongue is scouring the corners, the metal against me angled and cold, the taste of it the thing that keeps me from thinking of what is inside me, whether it still exists or has already dissipated again beneath this roof and in this posture of lowered head, my horns lightly bumping against the stall's fencing. When I lift them and step backward for a moment I cannot feel it – there is none of the hot spinning in my chest or the lightness in the flesh around my bones, until I look at the fence ahead of me, the same part that my horns were forced to rub against as I drank, and seeing this wall, this barrier I know that the power, the beginning of violence has not left me, I have not lost it in the gloom of this stall but have it breathing within my breaths, even now leaning its weight against my heart to start pushing the blood into the back of my head, the heat there a welcome burning, a fire that has always licked at the wood of this barn but that before I stamped at.

And then, what heat was it that I was afraid of? I feared the destruction of the things around me: to lose the rhythm between barn and paddock, the unclear gaze to the farmhouse and its gardens, the clearer sky above. These things I sought to protect, to nurture as if they were alive, unaware that the real life was twisting inside me and each raising of my head to ache my neck only pushed it deeper, the futile slow grazing and drinking of things around me giving only flickering moments of suspicion, seen in the suns of the boy's eyes, that the weight of my flesh was not merely a burden, and so I clung to the rutted paths that would take me from barn to paddock, to the hope that I would be left there to watch the night form its blackness across the sky, unable to let the blood rise higher than my withers because I did not know it could – I did not know it could! But now there is no suspicion, only nearby echoes and the images of things I have done: feelings within me of charge and impact, of what it is to choose the destruction of something and the joy of pulling the air and the ground around this chosen object closer, to have sensation explode in every part of me when before was a dull flatness like that of the ground beneath my hooves, pressed down on, immoveable until a seedling parts it.

My hooves clop quietly on the dark floor of the barn, a steady walk, a rounded path within the straight sides and corners of the stall, one eye looking at the walling and fence next to me, the other twisting around the same space until I am standing deep in my stall but looking to the other side of the barn where the horse is, and who if I lift my head I can see, the grey sculpture of his own head held high and watching me, his mouth unmoving and his ears alert. I walk forward and watch the fence quickly rise to hide him, the same slow clopping beneath and the sound of my breath escaping in a snort before I trot forward with head lowered into the fence, hitting it more with my skull than with my horns, feeling the wood bend and hearing small parts of it break, leaning forward to have it bow further and creak against my weight before stepping backward to pull my head free of it.

Through a gap the Grey is visible, the opposite stall's fence no longer pressed against his chest, a snort issuing from his own nostrils and his head making a short quiver with flattened ears as he takes another step back. As if to mirror him I step back as well, the wooden structure receding and becoming sharper before me, thin and weak angles of wood crossing over each other, in some places with order, in others like the chaotic growth of something old and dying, but all of it little stronger than the stems I have crushed into the earth – and I skip forward, raising my head and then bringing it down to smash at the fence, a horn catching in something, the structure creaking and snapping as I work at the wood with all my weight, a looseness ahead as something breaks before another part of it clings on to stop me. I pull back to hit it again, it spiked somewhere on my horn and the whole thing coming back with me before I throw myself forward to break more of it, the tension present as the fence holds but then gone as it releases its grip with a muffled crack, my head and neck pulled to the side and back as my body bursts first through the scraping wood onto the walkway between the stalls – I heave and swing my head free, a tangle of wood and wire flung from my horn to crash loudly somewhere unseen.

The ground beneath me is the same, it is no different to my hoof and leg, but to stand in this walkway facing the door at the end of the corridor with its thin strip of light I am aware that everything is changing, that the horse in his stall to my

side is not the same creature of bobbing head and a flash of
teeth even though he does these things now, and I turn my head
slowly to look into him, this new thing, to see the light grey
shape flickering through the gaps of the fence as it paces from
one end to the other, skidding as it turns, its head jolting down
with imbalance and then pulled up sharply as it stumbles over
the mess of wood and wire that was thrown from me. The
horse passes near and I feel the air of its movement, the smell
of its sweat punching through the holes of the fence to hit me
in nose and flank – I step closer so that the end of my snout
nearly touches the wood, a quick jerking movement that the
horse senses as if it has been struck, it still rushing from end
to end but now deep in its stall away from me. I watch its movement and know that I have caused this, that I have made this
shape that I can see in the gloom, a bright clarity in its distressed
pacing and turning, a beauty that makes me jerk my head from
one hole to the other so that I can have more of it, feel it filling
me with an excitement and a lust for what I felt before, a clop
from my own hoof as I stamp quickly lost in the many from
the stall in front, the stall carved out of the darkness by another
thin line of wood and metal: the fence; another fence before
me to be broken.

The horse turns again and seeing the sudden curve of flesh made by its neck and chest I am pulled forward and into the fence, the wood softer than that of my own and quickly bending inward, the horse rearing silently and flashing a hoof, shaking its head and spitting air from its nostrils before landing with a clack to retreat further into the stall, its breath and twisted pacing the things I hear most as I push into the structure at my head, rocking my weight into it so that it bends further and creaks with each movement, its rotten base where the Grey's urine has drenched it a growing weakness that I feel through my horns and neck until the whole thing falls over and into the stall and I stagger forward, my hooves catching in the lattice, tripping so that I fall onto it and am prone while the horse screams for the first time, bucking with a long hind-leg kick out to the side.

But I find the ground in between the wood beneath me and push myself to standing, the fence broken and useless and pressed down by my hooves, the horse panicked and frenzied and filling my eyes and ears with an awareness, a clarity that I stand and measure for an instant before picking my way over the ruined fence, deeper into the stall towards the horse that twirls in the corner and rears with the wall of the barn at its

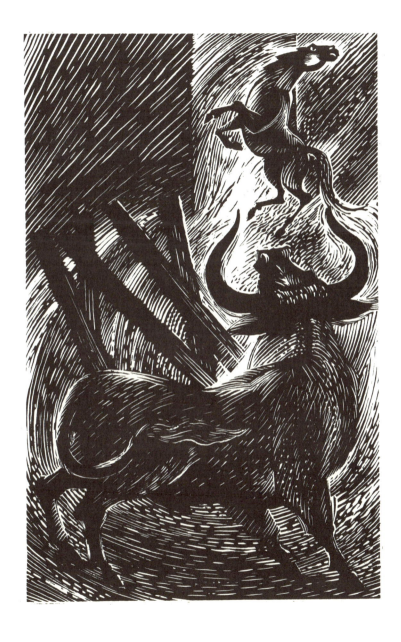

back, landing down on its forelegs with another scream, each movement and sound before me, every twitch and flicker made by the horse a thing that I have done, that I have made and is feeding me but makes me hunger yet, the tightening in my chest and the heat around my head held back as if on the edge of something – of my whim – and then the release: the pure release as I prance forward and smack into the horse's side, pinning it and feeling the firm barrel of its body rippling between my head and the wall, its neck and head a visible flailing in my eye.

I pull back and for a moment we both stand and breathe, close to the other, the horse's head stopping its movement and hanging low on its neck as if about to eat, while I stare blankly at its flank, a large grey shape very close to my eyes and nose. There is the smell of blood and the sound of it dripping on the floor, but I see no mark, no puncture in the grey before me where the horn went in – then suddenly I feel a rush of air and the horse is no longer there, the darker wall remaining, a disordered sound to my side that I turn to, watching patiently as the horse scrambles over the carcass fence and onto the walkway, trotting quickly down it towards the thinly open door, a space I cannot see from where I stand but that must not be wide enough for him to fit through because I can still see him – his head appearing and disappearing at the part of the fence left standing, his silent pacing at the exit crossing the bar of light cutting through the doorway to make it flicker and blink.

It was nothing – what I have done – a dreadful ease to create these fallen tangles of wood and the injured whirling of the Grey at the end of the barn. And now it feels as if it is passing: the hot layer into which I raise my head and horns and that drove me forward into wood and flesh dissipating in this quietness, an emptiness that has flowed from the air around me into my body so that suddenly I feel a great fear, a cold vibration of my insides and a shaking of one leg. I snort to try and spit it out through my nostrils, stamping the leg that trembles and then walking forward, the air becoming a pressure at my ears and chest, a tightening thing that makes me stagger over the wooden lattice in the stall and onto the walkway, the Grey becoming visible at the end of it, no longer pacing and turning but standing still, its neck held straight out from its back and its flank twitching, and now a dark patch visible, darker than sweat. I turn my head to see it in both eyes, the horns stopping to point in its direction, the long corridor of the walkway a thinning path to this figure of heaving breaths that the slash of light from the doorway tries to cut in two. But a single step towards him stokes nothing in me, gives me nothing but a greater and more slippery emptiness, a thing I know must be filled with something, and I turn away from the horse and to the ruined fence of my own stall, picking my way over it, stumbling through it until I am once again surrounded, the hole I have made hidden behind me.

But it is not enough to stand here, to collect the thoughts that come to me, because they die as soon as I think them, as if each time the bull inside me tries to raise its shadow head, a sun appears to destroy it. The looseness of the wood breaking, the feeling of the Grey's body rammed between my head and the wall are still there inside me, but not something to delight in, as if they were forced upon me and I did not choose them – yet I know I did. And suddenly I feel a remoteness to the things that before I cherished, a yearning for their structures that are not already lost, that I have not already trampled with this fever. I move to stand before the door that would lead me to my paddock, hoping that the boy or the man will let me out, staring at its blank and darkened wall but hearing no footsteps or the creaking of hinges, just my breaths and similar noises coming from the end where the horse is.

And even as I stand now, wanting to return to my paddock and move away from what I have done in the barn, I feel the falseness of this desire, the futility of waiting for one of them to open the gate, when with a lowered head I could easily open it myself. But to crash through the gate would mean to again choose freedom, a path that seems to have no comfort and scares me now – and perhaps I do desire to be in the paddock, to re-establish the web-like threads between my lazing senses and the things around me, the cords that before have held me firm. But I cannot do that here standing in my stall as I have no store of them. There is only the recent memory of sensation and violence, loud and violent itself and clamouring for the surge forward to smash the gate, an urge I do not know whether to deny or indulge, but the prospect of which does stir me, may yet lift me again, and I walk my heavy flesh around the stall to take myself away from the gate, the ruin of fence that I have made passing beside me, a glimpse of the horse's darkening form beyond it and then I turn towards the gate and skip forward and charge, an act made in uncertainty even as I lower my head and punch through, the wood dry and splintering around me, bright daylight above and the fences suddenly at both my flanks as I run down the rutted channel and follow its curve out into my paddock, a place I enter at a gallop and know is for ever lost to me, has died to make me storm back and forth within its confines as if to look for what has killed it, what has taken it from me.

But there is nothing present here but the noise I make: a low pattering of hooves on earth and stone that has no menace, no excitement, and soon I have stopped, alone in the paddock, breathing in the hot air of the afternoon. Around me there is silence and no movement, no flicker of dog or even bird, an emptiness not uncommon but which now emerges starkly and I swing my head from side to side to view it, taking a few irregular steps or turning – movements that do nothing to alter the expanse of baked scrub. I have no desire to look at the things in my paddock, to carefully walk its area and attend to what I see because I know it is all squashed and broken, and I break more of it each time I stutter forward and look to the horizon, the land beneath it still empty and silent while the sky it meets a solid sheet of blue.

I know that when this blue turns to purple and the stars begin to show I will not look to them, I will not see them as the bearers of any significance because how could they be? Unless the shapes seen there drop from the sky and present themselves to my horns I have no need for them, no wonder for some-thing I have made but cannot now destroy. For even though I wanted to stand in this paddock again, it was not from a hunger to regain or rebuild what was lost, but to know fully that it has gone.

Later, when I turn my head and can see a darkened sky to one side, the reddening sun to the other, there is a moment of nervousness when the first star appears, as if it might still have the power to engross, but it does not.

CHAPTER 9

Even as evening strengthens and more stars emerge my head is not pulled upward. The thing that turns me is a distant noise: what must be the labour of a vehicle as invisibly it approaches, the sound becoming louder – but seemingly as slowly as the day is darkening. I turn to face the distant curve and fold of scrub where I know it will appear, the path where they all appear and leave by and that will finally snake past the other side of the barn to the house – and when I do catch sight of it it has progressed further than I thought: a small dark shape with its noise in pursuit, the lights of its front not yet bright in the dusk. I watch as it comes closer, growing from a small dark spot like a crawling insect to emerge as something large and moving very quickly; feeling only a vague interest at its novelty as it passes out of sight behind the barn in a tumult of dust and flying stones. For a moment I am paused, as if listening for an impulse from within, before suddenly I am trotting quickly over to the part of the fence from where I can see the house, the vehicle stopped before it, one that I do not recognise and that the man has come out to meet, an eagerness in him, his hand raised in the air.

The sound of a foot scraping on the ground turns my head to the barn and there is the boy, standing at the end of it, looking towards the house and holding something that he rests on his shoulder, and that his whole body seems to lean against, as if pulled up and strengthened by it. He raises his free hand in imitation and I look back to the house where a second man has appeared, a figure I do not know but is of interest for the few sand-like grains of fear he puts in the bottom of my lungs, him and the man now walking towards the boy together but with very different gaits – as if they are different creatures, one resident to the terrain they cross, the other unfamiliar and picking up his feet like a cat through mud. When the three meet I hear their voices, quiet and lacking in spirit. Then they walk towards the barn and disappear behind its end – I hear the sliding of the door and know that they have gone into the hot stench and darkness, that they will see together the destruction of the fences, the wounded horse.

Suddenly the man has reappeared and is walking back

towards his house, a hurried pacing, his hands as fists and moving little by his sides as he pounds his way stiffly over the ground. I am watching him as he goes, my neck turning slowly to follow his movement, jolting back to the barn when I hear the boy and the stranger emerging and calling loudly, the tones of their voices filled with insistence and pleading to the one that seems to flee them, who has disappeared into the house when I look back up to it, quickly reappearing with a long object he tries to free from a covering even as he walks back down, his hands scrabbling at the brown hide until a dark glinting is released from it and the covering discarded to fall to the ground.

The boy and the stranger have walked part of the way up towards the house and are in the path of the man as he storms back down to the barn, making the weapon he holds click and jump in his hand as he goes – the same weapon I have seen him carry when he returns with rabbits strung upside down at his waist, parts of them missing, as if they were born without heads or a certain limb, or the huge wild pigs and their dead weight that he and the boy struggle to extract from the back of the vehicle. And I know that this walk he makes to the barn has the same intent of slaughter, but one that he does not seem to enjoy as he does the others, as if he is forced to take his quick stiff steps towards the long shadow the barn is casting out to him.

But he is not there yet, and heads for the boy and the stranger where they stand, as if to part them unthinkingly, but they do not move and instead block his way, their voices suddenly rising, their arms on him to hold him where he stands while he screams back and struggles with shoving movements of the gun so that locked together the three of them stagger and go nowhere, scratching at the earth with their feet. I watch, enthralled at this strangeness, aware that something else is watching when from the edge of my sight there is movement and I look up to see the woman standing in the doorway of the house, bending slightly as she looks at the men. Now the stranger's voice can be heard most of all, a steady stream of noise, not loud but becoming clearer, and their struggling ceases and their feet move less against the ground, this voice rhythmic and deep toned so that we all seem to be listening to it, even the paused insects – but the man most of all, whose face is so close to the stranger's that he must feel the other's breath.

Then all three seem to relax as if from some signal. Their hands stop gripping and shrink away from each other as they separate. The man and the boy stand and watch as the stranger walks slowly up to his vehicle, and I hear his voice and the woman's as they call greetings to the other, the man opening the vehicle so that it disgorges a large dark box, his voice and the woman's audible again as he turns with this thing carried at his side and begins to walk down towards the barn. He passes the man and the boy, saying something and waving his hand at them, which seems enough to keep them rooted to where they stand, merely watching as he continues down to vanish into the barn. Now for the first time the man turns and looks in my direction, the boy's head revolving shortly after so that they both face me, and I watch as their bodies turn and they begin walking over the rough ground towards my paddock, their pace languid, their postures and movement giving away no intent, but the woman is still watching them from the doorway and what must she see? She must see the backs of her two men receding towards the dark pit my flesh makes on the landscape, the spikes of their guns poking from shoulder or waist, the sun now reddening the sky to make the light slash sideways across everything.

They have reached the fence and we regard each other, the man and the boy before me, peering through the light that strikes them full in the face and gives them an orange and yellow hue, and everything behind them the same stain. They are close enough that I can smell them strongly and they could reach out and touch me if they wished, and the man does, not with his hand but with a step forward and then the long snout of the gun poking through the wire, an appearance I do not flinch at, I do not blink at as the large single hole hovers before my eyes and then presses against my head, the cold of it beginning to seep through to my skin, more so as the man seems to lean against the gun as if to drive its point into me – but which does not move my skull a fraction as I look to him and his snarl and the orange glow of his teeth. The boy next to him is relaxed as he stands there motionless and at a slight angle, the weapon he carries still resting on his shoulder, his head bent towards me and his eyes flitting eagerly between the man at his side and the large head behind the fence. There is none of his wildness, nothing the man must control, and without this barrier it seems the man's hate has no refinement and is pure and solid, and I feel all of it, every breath and twitch he makes flowing from him down the rod he tries to force into my head.

And it is not unpleasant, this pressure between my eyes, nor is the grimace and tremor of the man at its end, who must feel

he is pushing against a wall, or the ground itself and not something standing on it. In the distance behind him there is a sound:
a very low murmur that must be another vehicle approaching,
which these two before me do not hear because they do not
respond or move – and this immobility of theirs suddenly makes
the coldness pressed against my head an irritation: I lift my
neck slightly and this is enough that the man must step back,
the gun jumping to jerk his hands and arms back into him, his
teeth and anger suddenly replaced by a jolt of surprise, even
fear perhaps in that face of his as he senses the power, the
strength of the thing he hates, strong enough that a twitch of
its muscle can split him from his abhorrence and into fear.

The woman calls loudly, her voice like that of a bird's and
sharp enough to cut the man's eyes away from me, to make him
turn as the boy does to see a new thing: a vehicle – giant in
both length and height and lumbering along the path to the
barn, hidden by it briefly before reappearing and stopping to
hiss at its entrance. Its bulk, angular like the barn itself, sits there
at rest and we watch it, the glass at its front dark and reflecting
the red light of the sun, its long metal sides an incomplete skin,
punctured with slats and holes in an orderly symmetry – and
in one of these apertures I see a darker hole that I realise is the

nostril of something pressed against the structure, sliding along its edge as it tries to suck the smells of outside into it before retreating back to the darkness. Now there is movement behind the expanse of black and orange translucence at the front of the vehicle. The side of it opens and a figure emerges to climb out and jump down heavily to the ground, the door slammed shut by him to send a loud report rippling out over the near-silence of the scrub. He begins his way towards us and as he moves I see he is large for a man: his steps are laboured and already his mouth is open and panting silently, his arms swinging a little out to the sides with each step as if to throw his feet forward.

I look to the known man near me and see no eagerness in him for this creature – the boy too merely standing there and watching him so that the three of us are as blank as stone as he approaches. He looks up from the ground he struggles over and calls a greeting and the man utters one back, a small sound made with little breath while the boy stays silent, and when I look closer at the boy in curiousness it seems that he is repelled by this man, as if he can smell blood on his large and sweat-drenched frame and recoils from it, his body tensed and leaning back, his face high and averted – and suddenly I feel a real and far from phantom fear that floods my lungs to stop the breath that has indeed smelt blood: the blood of my kind, spiralling off the fat of this creature and into the air as if he surrounds himself with a herd of slaughter.

When he has finally reached the other two and stops to straighten, I watch as his hand rises and is a motion in my direction, his voice breathless and his eyes surveying me so that I see myself in them clearly: the curving black shape with earth and red sky behind it, standing quietly, only a slight movement of ear or tail. The fear is still there sitting beneath my lungs, but is changing and has already passed into something that is leaving me, that exists less with each breath I pull in above it, drawing in more of the scent of mixed bloods from the man, but which are not the thing I am afraid of. I know that what streaked through me was not the smell of death and gore that this man has rolled in, but shock as if at the final slumping of a burning structure, because I can sense from the way their low voices cross over each other like a snake its own body some exchange is being made, that the barn and the things I have stored from what I have seen is now only smoking black ash around my hooves, the three of them looking at me so that I know I will leave this paddock, that nothing of my previous rhythm, of the building of empty shapes, will remain.

And knowing this I feel my flesh becoming light again, not the burden that the return to the paddock threatened. Already the weight was beginning to press down on me as I stood here, quietly watching these men arrive and milling before my fence, listening to their voices and taking interest in their gestures – a tired mockery of a former stance – when my real desire lies in moving them myself, in hearing their voices raised and frantic rather than this warbling they give and take from each other. The three of them are still standing before me, the largest of them directly ahead, the man and boy loosely at either side as if drawing back, the fence of wire and post running between us, but suddenly no longer there. I look and cannot see it – there is no shining of wire, no post rammed down into the cracks, nothing but air and earth to separate me from this target and I burst forward, the ground moving beneath me to bring them all closer but mostly the largest one in the middle, the one whose bulk I want to feel thrown into the air by my own and who is stepping back in shock with his arms raised. But then I am slowing and cannot move forward any further: there is a cutting at my head and across my snout, my head is forced to turn to the side as I drive forward with my legs, another slash at my head so that I must close an eye, the other eye open and seeing one of the posts free from the earth and wobbling above the ground, the wires running tautly from it back up to this eye, up to my head that presses against them.

I have not stopped completely: I still creep forward and can feel perhaps another post coming free, a twanging pulse travelling along the wire from the side I am blind to. The men – now their voices have changed and I listen intently to their shouting: the newcomer afraid as he backs away in front of me, the man at my side calmer but still with fear as well and I realise he shouts something to the boy because the boy has moved quickly, swinging the gun from around his arm so that it rests against him and he can look down along its length. There is a small noise like something snapping and I feel the lash of a wire as it breaks and its end slashes at me – another snap and a prickling at my withers, not a wire but the product of the boy's intent, the dart there sitting with its long metal sting inside my flesh, a thing that feels very distant and small, but that is felt despite the sharper slicing of wires across my head and snout. I still push, forcing myself against the invisible web that has me tangled, the heavy man taking small steps backward and calling to the others – who reply repetitively like dogs: but dogs who are calming from a lessening threat. And then I find that I am not pushing, that I do not press forward with either leg or neck and have stopped; that I must stop and just lean against the fence and breathe, and suck the air into me.

There is movement, but it is without form except for indistinct shadows flashing in the low-cast light. I realise that the men and the boy must be moving about me, that they are the source of the black shapes that come up to my eye and yet I cannot see, and they are also making the noise of their voices, growing more meaningless and distant, as if the light streaming out across the ground from the sun is something thick and liquid and carrying them away from me. The wires of the fence press against me, across my snout and the top of my skull, no longer sharp or slicing but merely a thing that means I cannot move forward or raise my head, and when I think that to move my head might ease my breaths, it is like remembering something long forgotten to step backward, to feel the wires peel off me and emerge from my skin, the post to my side lowering from its suspension to land briefly upright before I watch it topple and fall, and then the last of the wire slipping free from my horns.

Now I stand breathing, another flattened fence before me, the figures beyond it unprotected, available were I to pick my way forward over the gold and curving filaments draped over the ground – and yet I cannot because there is no impulse in me, there is no desire to even want this impulse, to turn my head or eyes in search of it. Even to lift my head from the ground is an effort, as if there is a part of me trying to keep it lowered and that must be fought with – that I struggle against with long breaths and the pushing of my forelegs into the ground, to find that when finally lifted my head is shaking, that tremors run from my horns into my neck so that the earth and everything on it also trembles. The men and the boy seem to stand as before, a rough line of three shapes shifting in and out of the terrain behind them, the red from the sun deepening so that everything is made of blood-red light and black shadow. In an instant my head feels as if it will fall and I take a staggering step forward – a sound floating around in the air before I realise it is attached to the man, calling to the boy again and who I turn to just as he is lowering the gun from his shoulder, another needle lodged in my hide, the popping sound to start its flight heard separately, a thing detached and very distant.

Then my hind legs are no longer straight, bending beneath me so that I am half-splayed in the dust, sitting there like a dog might, my head still shaking and held out from a straightened neck. The paddock around me, the figures in front are moving up and down with the speed of a bird's flight and I close my eyes to block this, opening them a moment later to find the sun has disappeared, that there is only the twilight left from the pale sheet of sky above and the men and boy have moved away, have retreated to stand down near the barn where the boy has the Grey's bridle in his hand, is holding the horse while the other three men stand around it, the man I know turning away from the animal they inspect so that his head is a pale orb in the gloom facing up to me or beyond me, the boy behind him leading the Grey towards the vehicle, a lameness in the movement of its long legs. The large man follows the boy and the horse and together they cross the head of his vehicle, turning around its front corner to disappear behind it.

I move to stand, leaning forward to free the weight that presses my hind legs down, shifting them under me until I can push upward into a wavering stance to find that I cannot move my head, that it seems fixed as if the evening air is solid and my horns are stuck in it. Then I feel them: the long snakes of rope coiled around the base of my horns, their thickness weighing dully on the top of my head and across an ear, running out from me to end in several places in the ground so that again

I am trapped by cords, standing beneath their tension, hearing their fibres creak with every small movement of my head, every breath I pull inward.

I hear the man's voice calling the boy and look to see him coming towards me, deep disinterest for him or for the ropes still washing around my blood so that there is no heat in it, no flooding of it into my head and neck as together the man and the boy come up, the boy holding a large stick as thick as his arm, the pair of them skipping over the broken fence, moving quickly to find the ends of the ropes that hold me, which they release from where they are staked in the ground. Then I am pulled. The man is tugging me down towards the gate while the boy is behind me, the ropes he holds slapping against my side – and I hear the swish of his stick through the air and the other sound it makes as it hits me on the bone at my hind, a dull feeling there, neither painful nor pleasant, and when it comes again something makes me step forward, an unknown impulse that I know I should not concede to but that I must, because there is no need not to, no desire or force anywhere in me and even though my heart twists painfully around this step I am as bound to it as the rope is around my horns, I can only follow the man, watching him as he unlatches the gate and kicks

TAURUS

it open, walking through it onto the soft ground away from the paddock that is an unknown void behind me.

There is the swish and smack of the stick on my rump, and I realise that I have stopped, the man tugging at the rope, joined by the fat newcomer who also holds a rope and with his weight can pull enough to tilt my head. Perhaps I have stood here for some time: the muscle and bone at my hind does now hold pain, and the shouts of the men and boy are harsh and urgent as if they struggle. I begin walking forward again, my body heavy and a sleepiness around my head so that each step is a confusion, as if I am falling and only move a leg to stop myself tripping, the sounds in my ears shifting and blinking like the darkness that crosses my eyes, that must be the lids there closing, opened by the distant impact at my rear to stagger forward again down towards the barn.

And when we have reached the vehicle in this stuttering way it seems it faces me, its large head poking from its even larger body, shapes like eyes beneath the swathe of dark window but all of it wrong and angular, another confusion of shape, of sight and the sound of the men who are now side by side and pulling their ropes to get me round the front of the vehicle, to pause and step down its long high side, smells leaking from the holes and gaps there and the smell of metal beneath them all, as if I have dipped my head into a trough that holds them. I know that I should not be pulled like this, that a single yanking of the ropes around my horns would have these men on the ground and prone, that I might turn and face the boy with the stick and if he were to bring it down on my head it would do nothing to stop my charge for him – but these things, these shakings of the shadow bull's head inside me and the limbering of its neck and spine are too distant, starved of blood, as if a part of me cut off and lying on the ground, unattached to the heart that feeds it.

They have pulled me to the rear of the vehicle, where its ramp is waiting for me in a long sloping line down to the earth. Now the large man is moving up the ramp, the rope he holds making a slack curve from my head to his hand and I watch as he crashes up and into the vehicle, becoming unseen within its insides. I am not being pulled or beaten – I let my eyelids drop for a moment and then suddenly there is a whirring noise coming from inside the vehicle and I can see the rope rising from where it lay on the ramp, straightening as it is lifted, becoming taut against where I stand and then hauling me forward so that I stumble and lose my footing, my snout hitting the bottom of the sloping metal and the weight of my body pushing forward so that my head and an eye is pressed against it. But even as I try to uncross my legs from beneath me the rope is rigid again and pulling my head up the ramp, the rough surface pulling at the wire slashes across my snout so that I can feel grit and dirt collecting there like sand in a crack of earth – and feeling this I am able to think that at least I feel something, at least there is something still available to my senses, close enough not to be disfigured by my eyes and ears. I do not mind that the rope pulls me slumped and crumpled up the ramp, I do not try to stand or get my hooves beneath me because I have this pain to feed on, to blank out the disorder that surrounds me, and it is only when I am at the top of the ramp, the rope still pulling me upward and the sloping metal flattening out like a tongue into the vehicle that I have to stand, forced up onto my legs, the sensation at my snout dissipating so that I am invaded by the dark heat of the vehicle, throbbing out at me with a false presence so that I do not know where any edge or surface is.

I am pulled further inward, stepping blindly into the blackness, a slight twist of irritation for the tugging thing at my head and the noise it makes until it stops and there is silence. My head is immobile, held still by the rope so that I cannot move back and only a little slack with a step forward. I toss my head as if at a fly, the echo of irritation that has begun to creep back into my neck and back, that I examine to see if it is real, to see if I truly feel it. Then I see that the blackness to my side is incomplete – some of it is lighter, the openings to outside I saw earlier, and at that moment I hear a hoof on the metal and perhaps a snort, and know that neither came from me. And in this gap that I can look through I can see them: the men that hauled me down here, the heads obscured but their bodies and legs visible as they face each other, the larger newcomer giving something to the man who now is joined by the boy, something that he too is eager for, that they are both eager for as they stand there leaning forward, receiving it as I would the food in my trough.

But they are silent as they do this. Their voices do not slither over each other's as they did before, and suddenly the larger man has left them and a slight tremor passes through the metal at my feet: I hear the sound of the door closing, and then the coughing of the vehicle before its deep cacophony obliterates everything else. The man and the boy are standing and remain standing motionless as the vehicle lurches forward. I cannot see their heads but know they look, that they must watch as the vehicle leaves them with noise and rising dust, and when they have slid past the opening through which I peer, when the dark scrub begins sliding past to confuse me with its motion I turn my head away and feel the rope tense, and suddenly from the haze and confusion, from the slipperiness of my mind, I am considering its strength.

CHAPTER 10

For a moment there is silence. I can hear my own breaths: long sweeps of air turned one way and then the other and I listen carefully to this, these fragile sounds that are about to be roughly ridden over and then it comes again: the shouts of men, the scraping of foot and hoof against a flat dirt floor, the banging of a metal wall as large flesh moves against it. The floor beneath me is packed and hard as I step forward to press against the railings at the front of this stall that I am in – large and angular bars of metal making the heavy gate that banged shut behind me, that left me suddenly trapped with a stone wall in front, thick metal at my flanks and rear and just enough space to turn around without clanking my horns against the sides. The gate moves a fraction as I lean against it, a final solidity when it rests after this short looseness, and I wonder if my weight could push through it, the urge to do so a slow burning around my head, a fire put there by the rope that was tied around my horns in the vehicle, from which I could not break or free myself.

The gate does not move any further and instead I must feel its metal ridges scraping down my horn as I angle my head to look, to see what it is that suddenly screams and causes the men to repeat their own shouting, an increase in the banging and thudding against metal, sounds strange without their movement until I drop my head lower, below a thick band of metal, and can see down along the walkway, to where the large figures of men are hanging on to a gate like the one I look through, one of them holding a rope that I follow as it shakes its way up to the bridle of a horse, a dun creature that screams again and tries to buck its head against the rope, its eye white and rolling as it is held, a man hopping down from the gate and scooping something up from a pail on the floor, something that is dripping and breaks apart but that he takes with him as he climbs up, one hand reaching out quickly to grab the horse's ear, the other pushing this substance into the veined aperture to start the horse bucking its head again and kicking against the stall.

I watch; I cannot turn away. The noise and movement, the distress of this horse makes a vague excitement and a compulsion to observe inside me, a separate fire from the one in my neck and withers. The uncertainty of these new surroundings, the long path lined with stalls that I walked down before the way was blocked by the gate that shut me in – these things and the slight fear they have put in me are fainter feelings before the vision of this horse, thrashing against the gate, the sounds it makes slowly being muffled to itself by the clogging of its ears.

Yet turning away it is only the strength of the gate that exits, that means I cannot get at them: the figures just observed and the ones that occasionally walk past and glance in, the impulse triggered at their movement twisting inside me as if it will break the bones of my neck. I begin to butt the gate with my head, hitting it at all parts of its travel to create a dull thudding in my head and a metal clanking of my own – one that brings them to me: the men who were attending the horse, appearing separately to then stand together and look through the gaps in the metal at the bull they see within. I jerk my head and look to their eyes, lit by the blinking strips and bulbs hanging from the low roof, each of them studying my form, their voices quiet but with an eagerness that they do not hide or seem surprised by, as if they see something that they recognise, and welcome.

But they should have no thought for my nurture, to lead me

from here to another paddock and back again as they did on the farm, because my growth is complete. I have finished the accumulation of mass, and the greater task of observation, to not be fearful of the things around me. Here where the smell of blood comes off these men and is stamped into the ground beneath – here in this tunnel of stall and thin walkway there is nothing for me to protect, nothing that might be lost. And whereas before the sight of the men struggling with the dun horse would have gripped me long after the event – long enough that I could take it with me beneath a black sky and see it dance again in the lights there – now it has already left, a worthlessness compared to what I might feel, what I already know can be felt and which is now all I crave.

Suddenly my horns are rattling in the gate: I have launched forward, my awareness of smacking into the metal not arriving until after the act, as if trailing and then pulled on the end of a short cord. My forelegs paw at the bottom of the gate, looking for purchase, my horns are snared in the framework to bend my neck as I push upward while the men that I can see in both eyes have stepped back in unison, their voices light and playful with each other, watching as I struggle to get the gate off my horns and step back into the stall to ram it again. As I skip forward and strike it I feel the strength of the structure pass down me, the sturdiness of its joints to the metal walls at my side and their strength in turn – and this is a new sensation: this unbending firmness that both frustrates me and draws me forward so that I must ram it and ram it again, tiring little within a steady rhythm to pump a banging sound down in both directions of the tunnel, doing so until the men have fallen silent and sated have moved away, the last one remaining to watch and entranced enough that I can briefly see myself smeared across his eyes: a black ball of muscle unfurling to compress again against the metal structure, shaking it and the metal walls around it, stopping to breathe and eyes appearing from the darkness to look at the man who watches it before another surge forward.

Soon he too is gone and I am alone, a deep quiet between each thud I make against the gate, a meaning to these divisions of silence that I become only slowly aware of: that I am truly alone within the long tunnel, and I stop ramming to listen to their absence – the men, the horse – there is nothing here but me and the flickering and buzzing lights strung down the ceiling, some listless insects colliding with them. I walk slowly to the gate and peer down towards where the horse was but it is gone, no sign that it was ever there, too much overlapping scent for it even to remain as one. And the other way along the tunnel, the way I came down with lust but uncertainty before entering this stall – I look that way also and there is no movement, no sign of the other beasts I passed in that fast trot down, flashes of eye and horn behind metal, their heads at strange angles as they watched, the twin salience from their heads at stranger ones.

I do not know what I have missed, what has passed me as I rammed the gate, lost in the repetition of the act. Did I see dark shapes flash across my sight, the sound of hooves skittering down the walkway? And it is not silence that I stand within. If I am still and unbreathing there is a sound: a faint murmuring that seems to come from the stone wall behind me and the low rounded roof of this place, as if this stall and I stand within a long tube that has been stabbed into something alive – that something huge and living exists around it, above it. I raise my head and look to the roof, which is very close, unlike the barn, lights and their wires strung there imperfectly but what I see most is the roof itself: the grey and patching stone, darkened in places by moisture, solid and dead and yet resonating intangibly with life beyond it, as if I look at the exposed bone of something, aware of the blood beneath.

A sound to bring my head down and turn it: footfalls coming along the walkway, a solitary man appearing as a torso and legs and who does not continue past, instead stopping at my gate where I can see more of him through the railings, and smell him – he of the same smell and image as all the other men here that have been near me; I can find no difference between them. He walks slowly across the length of the gate until he is almost beyond the stall, then stops and lowers his head and raises his hands in a gesture I have seen countless times, the clicking sound in the gate or its post the prelude to its opening, that suddenly fills me with an excitement in my chest and legs and turns me to face where the gap will widen. The man moves back and the gate goes with him, his shield as I wait for the space to move through, to get out of the cramped stall and maybe charge, him now hanging on to and swinging with the gate so that he recedes from me with an alien smoothness, something I can only watch as he glides backward, the last of him the long stick he holds out and over the gate and that wavers when he and the metal stop abruptly to become a barrier across the walkway.

I step out, emerging from the close walls to create the long space of the walkway to one side, the metal gate and the man behind it to the other. He shouts and swishes the stick and again I recognise these gestures: suddenly this man has become the boy of the farm, standing on the fencing of my stall, urging me to go through the open door when for some reason I had remained there, rooted, perhaps by something seen or collected to turn my eyes inward, the cherishing of this figment the sideways movement of my jaw. But what was it then that I could have nourished, that could have occupied my mind so that I would not seek sensation? What was it ever that I could be so different to the bull that rages in me now?

And seeing the man on the gate who is not the boy I do not pause but turn from him and memory, to begin trotting down the path between the stalls, their closed metal gates a double fencing at my sides, but far enough apart that they do not touch my flanks, the lights above meandering as if I stagger beneath their straightness. But I do not stagger, I am not uncertain as I trot down this channel, the hum of life falling from the roof like a rain to lighten my head and lift it, excitement a haze around my eyes so that it is as if I do not truly see where the stalls end or how I enter the chamber that I stop within, the roof suddenly far from my head, the walls less lit but visible as dull banks of stone, an angular smoothness surrounding me. I swing my head and see an opening in the wall to the side, a dark round hole with nothing visible within, the dull glint of metal across its lower half. And turning further with a new placement of hooves I see that I have come from a similar hole, the tunnel still lit so that the aperture is a glowing disc in the wall, the stalls and walkway visible as long lines tapering away to meet each other at its end, a tube of receding space quickly broken by the gate that swings out to bang shut across its lower segment. I turn again and there is a last opening, this one also illuminated, the same sucking sight of a tunnel disappearing into the distance and in this one at least there is movement that I can see through its gate: perhaps the high head of a horse in one of the stalls, the more definite steps of a man walking down the pathway, miniaturised by his distance.

I can feel my heart in my chest, beginning to smash the blood up into my head, my ears throbbing with the sound coming from above and a fury of indecision prancing me forward and around, towards the openings lit and darkened and away from them back into the chamber, the false and hollow desire to be back within that stall a thing I trample on, but that keeps rising in me with no other target, no alternative present. Then there is a noise: a loud and clear sound that dampens all other sounds,

like the call of a bird that can be heard even though it is high
above and there are other noises closer, that stops the movement of all the small things in the scrub. Before me suddenly
is my shadow, the clear outline made not by the dim lights
above but by the sun itself, and I turn to see the last of an
expansion: a large space of brilliant daylight extending at the
sides as if stretched, two quiet thuds from either side as this
ends and leaves an open space before me that I explode towards,
my hooves cracking at the firm dirt-ground until I am out of
the chamber and on softer sand, a rushing and bellowing of
sound around me, coming from all around to drown the bird-
like song, as if the air I move through is thick with life that is
suffering as I part it.

I halt and bring my head up, plumes of bright sand shooting
forward from my hooves and up to speckle my chin. The smell
of blood is strong and the sun is suddenly a great weight above
me: I can feel its power trying to push me down, the eye of
this huge and breathing animal that I suddenly find myself in
the centre of, it moaning and roaring as I bring my head down
and charge one way and then the other looking for its flank,
looking for contact with its mass which I can feel all around
me and yet not puncture, as if within it there is only the space

of my form that it can allow, but that shifts like air to flow around me, to evade my horns.

I stop again to breathe and raise my head, the heat inside my veins and flesh far hotter than the sun, blocking its gaze that seemed to blind my own so that suddenly I can see the curved wall encircling me, the tall bank rising up behind it and something distinct to direct my head and horns: a sound, a young voice, slicked with elation and excitement at what it sees before it and I look to the wall expecting to see a head perched there, instead seeing for the first time that the bank that rises behind it is alive, is the shifting and writhing insides of this beast that roars and screams around me. Its skull and heart I have seen, and now here is its open flank, a thing that I must run for, a desperate eagerness to get my head amongst it, to lift my horns with slithering and oiled entrails hanging from them and I burst ahead with all the pace I have, bringing the wall towards me, the red curve becoming smaller the closer I near it so that I feel a mere hop will have me over it and then I am pushing upward into the air, tucking my forelegs up to my chest, my hind legs straightening in an imitation – but I do not jump high enough and the wall suddenly expands to strike out and hit my shoulder, a crack and a dry splintering of wood,

I am not over it and remain in the ring, searching for breath, the wall at my side and my head turned in towards the open space.

And there in the centre of it where I have just stood, coming towards me, is a figure of light, a shining droplet from the sun suspended above the ground, darker legs appearing as it comes closer and placing steps deliberate and graceful, the light of it receding and in its stead a brightness of colour to lock my eye, as if a garden has been formed into a man and now approaches me, the last unfurling bloom the pink wing that sprouts from its chest to open with its lowest edge touching the ground. For a moment I am transfixed, unable to move before this wonder, an echo of my former and cold lust to collect such sights passing through me with a terrifying shudder, as if I will be sucked backward into a less-formed state, into my youth. Then I am pushing away from the wall on which I have been leaning and have started forward, scattered hoof-falls collecting into a gallop to bring this apparition and its bloom closer, a senselessness to the sound that is building as if my own openings have been blocked, and I do not even care for sight as I lower my head to bring the heated points downward, expecting impact: the jolt of something large to fall up and over my back. But instead there is a slight wind and a temporary darkness, a strong and sharp scent as I am enfolded and then emerge back into the sunlight, the feel of something stroking the back of my neck and withers but nothing ahead of me or stepped on beneath, and as I bring my head up to end the movement suddenly I know what it is that is done to me – memories strong and thickly solid as if stones to rattle in my chest of this feeling: of the long touch of fabric on my back, a ring like this one, men surrounding me with arms outstretched, held out and holding something draping like the young boy in the barn did – that I see as I turn and halt that the man before me does now.

I am compelled to drop my head and start forward, the air running over my neck and back, dimly aware of this sound and the wave of another from further away, bringing the space where the man last was towards me and again there is no impact but just the rustle of fabric passing over, a softness and pliancy in which I search for resistance with quick tossing and jerking movements of my head upward and to the side, finding nothing there but its thin lightness. A brief shade then I am out in the light again and feel the fabric running along my spine, lifting off with a crackle and the greater noise coming from the steepened bank, a thing again I turn to after stopping, it looming there protected by the curved wall, the slithering mass for an instant very clear as heads and eyes, limbs and torsos – and again I have the urge to be amongst them, to jerk and toss my head within them and I run for the wall, head raised, and able to see the beginnings of their scrambling to flee the part I head for, before the wall is suddenly very large in front of me and I know I cannot jump it, know it cannot be vaulted and must turn without leaping.

There is the man again, standing before me, the pink wing unfolded and quivering before him so that he seems to float above the dirt, his torso and head unconnected to the ground as he glides towards me and I step towards him, the noise there in my ears: shouts from the swaying heads and torsos in the banks louder as I break into a run with my head up to watch for him – louder still when I drop the horns to strike. And though I hit nothing but the bending wing that folds around me, it is the noise that is felt as I touch it, the power of the sound passing through me: a realisation that it is mine, that my movement is tied to it as if by ligament and each turn of my head or kick of leg will make it scream or howl. This storm of sound, it is a force beyond the mocking calls surrounding the ring of the farm, a place now overgrown and choked with weeds but that once held as pure a substrate as this – a sand that I passed over similarly cloaked by man, the repetition of this covering beneath the sun, no feeling of the body I knew to be near me at every pass until I slashed my head to the side and suddenly felt the light brush of true flesh against a horn, a distant memory that bolts through me now to snap my neck obliquely outward, the point still covered by the fabric but at its tip a slight pressure screaming back at me, the sudden tension of another's muscles beyond it as clear as if I am grinding the horn into stone. And there is a sound as I do this: the solid punch of air being blown out or sucked in through many mouths, a wall that I burst through and shatter as I come out again into the light, turning to see what is there and finding that the man still stands, his wing askew and his thin legs visible – and watching him as I suck the sound that is around us into my chest to quieten it, looking into his eyes I know that I caught him: a part of his body was for a moment at the end of mine and suffered from it.

I stand in the sun and feel it: the resistance that briefly passed down into my neck, the sound it made almost like thunder and with a few bird-like shrieks streaking through it. But nothing moves – or, startled, has taken to the air above me – and the memory is short and fading fast to become unpleasant, a thing that cannot be grasped and nurtured but only gives the scouring left by its passing, that begs me not to stand still but to move forward again, the legs of the man ahead quickly shifting before the wing comes down and they are masked, while the sound that was trapped in my lungs escapes to echo in the banks around us as I start forward again, keeping my head raised until I am almost upon him.

I lower my head and am shaded, the thing I rustle through suddenly an unbearable friction at the tip of my horns, points I rake to one side and then the other, searching for impact but finding none, emerging from this useless undulation of head and neck to find another man before me, the same image as the first. He too is covered by his half moon of colour and I think that it might be the same figure that has moved without me seeing, that disappears to appear somewhere else. But as soon as this figure moves I know it is not the same one. His movements are less graceful and more urgent, he steps before me and flaps the wing so that I see his legs appear briefly with each increment, a movement I know made to entice me, that sends pulses of heat up and down my spine and into my head and hooves, the only barrier to stop the burst forward the sound of footsteps behind me and that I turn to, where the other figure is walking away.

This man's back is before me, a small block of colour, the legs and arms sprouting from it, while above is the head with its dark extensions, as if a beetle about to take flight. But it is the back that I see, that my eyes are pulled to: the torso tapered at the waist, widening into the shoulders and between this an open area of body undefended, uncovered by the cloth he drags on the dirt – and though I hear the other one shouting at me, stamping for me to turn my horns to him, my head can only jerk quickly to the side, seeing him there as a flash of colour very close before I turn back to the man who walks away, who does not have his eyes on me. I am about to move towards him but then stop – there is something in front of me, a wall of memory that grips my horns as if they are in a sheet of stone, and I must stand and wait for its approach, for it to sink me into the ring of the farm, not overgrown but as clear and blood-less a canvas as the perfect sky above. I am there and yet I have not moved, can still hear the one to my side calling and scuffing the sand, the other in the same lift of a foot away from me.

Is this my blood, heated by the sun that has not shifted, leaking vapours, echoes of its past into my head? Again I turn to the annoyance at my side, the man so close that I can feel the breeze made from the wing he flaps at me, the greater hum from the banks settling on my neck and spine, as if it waits for their next flexing that is only the turn of my head towards the retreating figure. But a part of my youth is swilling in my head – and though I know it happened it may as well have been never felt. It exists only in flashes, in shudders as I stand here watching the man walking away, a form I myself have seen before because it was my body, my muscle and intent and not merely the memory of my blood that has run such a thing down and felt the horn shattering through the bone and muscle of its back. The vision of the boy of the farm, the images we shared, were not vapours or essences but our memories: the things collected through his eyes and ears, but for me a separateness from it all, the novelty and suddenness of that killing meaning that I could not gather it fully before it had passed.

How could I not feel then what would only be felt later? I must have been somehow dead, somehow asleep to the ground and sky that I stand between now, the heat in my skull suddenly like fire around my eyes, thick sears of heat and pain bolting through me as I realise what I have done, what I have forgotten. Because it was the boy that felt that day, not I – he that took away what he saw to nurture his own formation while I was returned to the adjacent structure: the barn, my stall, to the darkness there where I could not see or hear anything, where the scant memory of that event was lost in the repetition of the walk to the trough for food or water, the sudden light of the opening door: more sustenance brought piled in the barrow by the boy, his eyes aglow, my gaining of flesh and weight resumed without interruption bar the travelling through the channel of wood to the paddock: to sometimes find another there, no phantom threat or mirage enemy but another body like mine, the large eyes watching me approach, the horns mere stubs from its head.

Now I stand in this ring, my own horns freed from the stone that held them, a sudden looseness in my neck as memory disperses. The man that I watched has become distant, is approaching the curved wall where heads similar to his are arrayed atop it. I swing my neck to the one that is nearer, uncertainty shaking my head at the end of this movement. He is still very close and available were I to plunge forward – and as if to trample this hesitation I dive towards him, a quick advancement that draws out a sound as if I pull a root from the earth: a dwarfing resonance as I lower my head and gouge sharply to one side and then the other, looking for the solid enemy beyond the drape.

Then I have emerged with nothing but the light whip of air and fabric leaving my haunch, no pressure having been felt to pass into my neck. I turn, twisting my hooves in the sand and dampening the sound around us with this movement, a dull anger firing up and down my spine that I cannot make contact, that means I cannot pause after turning and must immediately charge again, dragging the sound with me as if it trails from the horns that I lower, towards the figure who is closing. Another slashing sideways movement of head, another emergence to turn quickly and tightly again and repeat this searching until I have become desperate and frenzied, frustrated by the loose cloth, spiralling in a tight circle to jar the bones in my legs. I know he is very close, can feel him brushing my side as if we spin around each other in these passes, but suddenly I feel a hunger in my lungs, an urgent need to fill them and I must break off and stand to pant, the colours of yellow sand and red wall sharpening in this stillness, the figure to my side a dazzling slash of light and pink, the dirty grey innards above the wall rising up before the membrane of bright blue sky seals us in. The figure turns and there is his back – and though I heave for breath I am snapped forward by this sight, a quick movement swelled by the noise that I do not pull but pushes me so that I am almost on him as he turns; I see the ground moving quickly beneath me, the sand entering my nostrils as I feel the weight of something in one horn, a leg perhaps, a pressure I swing my head against before whatever it is slips off and I have a drumming against my flank, the light pattering of something imbalanced and revolving against me.

I raise my head, the blood there hot and pleasant – and as I begin to turn I see two figures before me, the same bright colours, the same annoyance of pink cape flapping towards me as they approach in a compact and sideways run, splitting to either side as if to part my decision, my choice that settles for the nearest and for whom I head, the noise still pushing me but like the rush of a liquid so that I slide on its surface, running towards him, and then the other that appears at an angle when I am out, my lungs empty of breath, until I stop and pull large gasps into my chest, watching as the several figures like a flock of birds scurry diagonally and start to vanish as they reach the wall, disappearing as if their bodies disperse against it to leave nothing but their misshapen heads: the beetles with their armour flared, perched along its edge. I stand and breathe, looking, wondering at the emptiness of the ring, the sand ablaze where I stand, a creeping shadow to halve it that is black to look at, the heat a sudden pounding on my back and flanks.

And from within the shadow, the black relenting to the hazy edges of unclear shapes, I find movement, a thing that must be alive but appears to have sprouted as if from the sand itself: a large mass of it coagulated by the wall and shifting. I step in its direction, interested, towards this new apparition and just a single hoof-fall forward allows its legs to form, the head and long neck to appear at one end while from its back bursts a torso with its own head – and arms, which through reins are sawing at the mouth so that the larger, eyeless skull is twisted sharply to one side and the other, blind movements of its legs responding with quick but uncertain placements to scrape the whole creature back and forth against the wall. I do not need to hear the metal clinking at its teeth, or look further to the fusion of its spines to know what grace might suddenly unfold from it, and I think with a growing excitement as I begin towards it that there is no fence between us, only the border of light and shade, a line I pass through to enter a delicate coolness, the creature before me reacting to the noise I stoke as my trot is eclipsed by gallop, the torso above it twisting towards me, more than just the reins in its hands, and as I near it I know that it will not move, it cannot evade me like the men, and lowering my head I smash its grace against the wall, feeling all of it pass down both horns and into my body, the shuddering of my own bones a glorious sensation; an eagerness to pull my head back to spring forward again at the bending ribs I can feel before me. With straightened legs I push my weight and horns into the creature's thick hide, an armour that flexes but does not puncture, sensing keenly the damage wrought beneath before I feel a sharpness in my shoulders: a pain and coldness, a welcome certainty there after the torture of the cape that flushes me with a quiet elation – because not only do I feel the mass at my horns, I also feel the spike of its defence: a tooth or blade that has split the skin at my shoulders to form a trickle down my flank.

I step back, the sharpness in my withers sluicing free, a mist of droplets before me that seems to ignite the air into a compressed roar, a noise that only increases as I charge forward again and feel myself clatter into the broad flank, bucking my head up against it, the horns catching or slipping on its hardened and ridged surface. The spike is at my shoulders, breaking the skin in a new place, a fresh pain and more liquid to start running down my neck, an anger at this puncture replacing the pleasure of its novelty so that suddenly I am pushing frenziedly at the creature, ramming it in short bursts from leg and neck that are sliding it along the wall, the stabbing point now scratching and slashing at my withers but not entering, unable to pierce the muscle and blades of shoulder that spasm at its tip. A further plunge forward and then I feel a weight beginning to press down on my head – suddenly the whole thing slides sideways as if attached and spun against the wall, the pressure lifting from my neck to become a large object on the sand beside me, a hoof at the end of a long thin leg hissing past my eye. I lift my head into the sheet of noise, a moment when I am paused without moving, listening, able to see the horse's dun stomach and a pair of legs parallel to the dirt, their opposites sticking in the air, its neck curled and the head with covered eyes forced onto its own flank, the reins from its grimace taut wires to the figure that is separating from its back. And even with the noise from the banks I hear its breaths, can see the dilation of nostrils as it pulls in its black and muffled air – and when I sense the men approaching me, see one of their heads behind the wall and fear they will take this from me, I drop my head and stab the horns downward, down and deep into the uncovered flesh, one horn glancing off bone until it is almost to the hilt, a hoof from the horse clattering against my skull to merely shake it, the figure that tried to split from it sometimes visible when my head jerks up: a lighter coloured flailing trapped between horse and ground.

Then one of the men is very close at my side. From the corner of my eye I see him moving, flapping and hopping and his voice a clearness, a call to the blood that is raging in my head and seeping from my shoulder so that I do not control the movement in his direction: I concede without hesitation to the raising of head, the quick shuffling of hooves to turn, matching his own rapid footfalls and then the charge forward to where I thought he was, the current of air from his cape rustling over me – and then I am standing uncovered and panting. The noise has lessened, a patience that I inhale, my blood still resonant with what has happened, what was felt and is shuddering through me so that I am content to stand and live from it, my head making tiny jerks at the air ahead as it feels the echo of each impact, every glorious contact, an immersion of many long breaths in this rich liquid until I look across to where the horse lies, to find another pair of horses unarmoured and harnessed standing near it, and the anxious scurrying of men like angered insects as they attach some device of wood and metal between the two.

And if I turn the other way, into the crescent of sunlit dirt, I see arrayed there the men, their capes half draped at their legs, all of them facing me but unmoving. Even if they were to move, to goad me, I would not respond, because my head still vibrates with remembered jolts, my spine still feels its pure compression to banish any itching there. They have faded too, the men and the pink they hold – even the ground they stand on is duller, the red wall around them tinged with grey, as if the fullness of my skull as I stand here buffeted by recent sensation is enough to drive their luridness from my eyes. The low murmur of sound that has shifted in and out of my attention slants quickly into something with a keener edge, while below this noise there is a jangling of metal to the side, and I turn my head to see another deformation of the horse: the one I have upturned sliding over the sand on its back, its limbs kicking at the air as if prancing, the two horses in harness trotting before it and all of them being led by a man who runs by their side, who leads the trio into an opening in the wall, a dark and spacious gap that I look to and consider for an instant, something cold and very small streaking through my chest, a slight raising of my hoof before both the opening and what it caused in me have disappeared.

A man enters my vision from the side. Flapping the faded pink sheet he holds, his voice higher than the others, perhaps from youth, and I turn to him away from where the opening was in the wall, my head no longer quivering, able to see the unlined face beneath the black carapace that sits on his head. Memory has subsided: I no longer feel intensely what I have just done, it slipping away quickly and shockingly so that I am left with too much breath, an urge within me to have again, to recreate, moving my hind legs around so that I face this boy, aware that he will hide behind the thing he holds, thinking I will slash to the side as I did before, but earlier and with more violence, the sound suddenly weaving around the two of us and building as it follows the hot blood into my head.

But there is another sound – the unmistakable click of metal within a latch – a signal that forces my head to turn away from the boy to where the opening was, to find the creature of armoured horse and man reconstituted at the wall, facing me and for a moment moving forward with springing steps before its head twists around sharply, the dun fur turned to a grey stone, a limp in its gait as it turns its flank, the neck and curve of head obscured by the cloth at its eyes. But like the trace of smell that scrapes the barrels of my snout I know these things, I know these movements and the shapes that make them, I have sensed them daily and now here the Grey stands before me, fused to the spine and thick cladding upon him, his head violent and twisting from one side to the other, the whistling breaths from deep within him clear in the hush that my stillness commands.

I feel the urge to charge flicker in my lungs, my own breaths catching and uncertain, as if they must pass through a wet skin that covers my nostrils, which punctures and reseals with each column of air pushed through it because here is the past, altered but recognisable, the Grey's scent and movement spawning memories of what it is to be enclosed, safe within fences both real and fashioned – while behind him shuts an opening, the latch clicking, the promise of a darkness beyond where there are stalls and troughs, the rhythm that they bring. And though I have trampled and sought to destroy these things I find their echo haunting: glimmering with repetition, riddled and made sharper by the shame and weakness of my compliance.

The Grey is still twisting as I stand and watch, fighting the man that holds on to his mouth with the lashing of his head and neck so that they are often separate: the man's spine pulled from the horse's to slump back down on it, his arms jerking with the twanging reins, only the slightest agreement between them. The hooves below this struggle have revolved in their steps so that horse and rider stand before me in profile, and for a moment in stillness they meld, a single object against the dulling red wall, but with lines I have known disfigured by the false skin covering the horse, and a long stick speared through the man's chest before a quick movement releases it from under his arm to bring it slanting downward, the point a metal thing slashing at the air. In my chest and head throbs the impulse to start forward, and I wonder if I might stand here and let it boil to jet the blood from my shoulders, to savour fully the solidity that exists around my head, as if the sky has lowered to make even the air between us like stone, a rock that crumbles as my horns scrape it with the mere uplift of a breath. And I stand as if at the edge of something – my forelegs planted to keep me fixed, locked so that they spear into the sand and behind this the inexorable shadow within, pushing steadily and patiently until the feeling in my blood has become a certainty in my mind and I know that however much I might want to remain merely standing, there is no choice but to stagger into a slow trot, the long curved wall and the coagulation of horse and other in front of it suddenly distant, but closing.

As I accelerate, even then I think I might stop, that I might choose to suddenly fix my legs in the ground and feel the weight of my mass jolt forward – but this is an illusion, a thin tendril of will like the weakest feathered root of an upturned tree, no longer clinging to earth and useless, carried upward by a greater movement. The sound swells around me as I run faster, bringing the wall closer so that it begins to loom as a bending swathe of dark red across all my sight, the Grey in the centre of it and his legs a visible uncertainty as one hoof moves back and forward in repetition, while from his blinded head an arm has grown, the hand attached to the bridle and running up to a man's torso half-emerged from behind the wall. His tail sticks straight out behind, an oddness I notice even as I pace towards him until I see the hand and arm holding it, another torso and head poking above the wall to create a beast of many arms and legs, joined together to clamp this part of the wall, fixed to it and attached even to the rippling mass behind so that I do not only charge what is in the ring, but the greater being that spreads up into the banks, that has followed my movement with its noise – and at this prospect suddenly there is no ground, just my

JOSEPH SMITH

thunder over it until the flank and its human array is upon me and I am lowering the points, bringing them down at the very end of the movement, flushed with certainty as they strike the flank and burrow inward.

There is no breaking of the skin and yet my horns do not slip but move steadily with my weight towards the wall, the snapping of a rib felt like a distant sound, while closer the drier crackle of wood that I can feel near-bursting behind the chest I crush. Then I do feel a liquid, not at my head but at my withers to run down and gather at my stomach, the spike of this beast working its way around the flesh of my neck and near the blades of my shoulders, releasing the blood there, sending pain in rivulets out into my back and limbs. The noise clamours again to press down on us, a roar to echo the pain and the sudden anger that this pain and its edge of fear has placed in me. I take a single step back and raise my head, a horn clacking against something: the stick that has its end buried in my back and that my own movement levers upward, to tear the flesh there further.

With my eyes raised and sight widened I see a part of the Grey's sharply veined head and the sweated neck, the angle of these things twisted against the many arms that hold them to the wall, his visible nostril opening and closing with the ferocity of his breaths, as if he tries to make a sound: a scream or neigh into his own darkness. There are flecks of blood on the shin of his hind leg, and in a fresh writhe against the bridle his neck is twisted so that I can see a new wound, too high for my horn, a small cut made by something sharp at the base of its cheek – and seeing this incision I understand a thin confusion in the metal stalls before entering this ring: the flash of a light in the hand of one of the men as they stuffed the dun horse's ears to end its screaming; the blade he held suddenly inseparable from the silence of the Grey before me, the patient silence of the dun horse before him.

The signs of suffering are clear: I sense them all as plainly as I felt the breaking rib. But they are no barrier, they could never stop the short spring forward, an impulse that perhaps I own but more belongs to something else, so that it does not matter how much I truly will the lowering of my head to put it amongst the nervous hooves and spindle legs, to have them patter close to either eye, to feel the spike searching for me again before I tilt my head back and bring the horns straight upward into the Grey's belly, thinking I will topple it this way and startled by the sudden torrent of thick warmth that floods my ears and nose and clogs my eyes, the weight of the entire beast held in the width of my neck before it slides over to thump its flank against my spine, another separate and lighter impact at my hind: the man unseated, bouncing from me to the ground.

Slickened with blood, my head is sliding against the wall, my neck bent behind it, but I cannot move because the horse lies across me, as if a burden, his legs kicking out to clatter against the wood to make an irregular sound like the first giant drops of a rainstorm, heard on the roof of the barn. My own legs are half-splayed below me so that the sand is against my stomach, my breaths shortened and insufficient to feed the burning that starts in my lungs, squashed within their chest, the tubes that bring them air choking and coughing on the spattering of thick fluid sucked into them. I do not breathe, and in fear I try to draw my legs towards me – to get them underneath the weight in order to push upward – but it is not until the floundering of the Grey increases to a violent twisting pulse that he slides off my back and I can stand, a long scrape of one horn up against the wall, dragging my head against this friction until my forelegs straighten, convulsions of my own back and neck slipping my hind end free from the heap that pinned it.

The curve of wood stands against my flank, a solidity that in my search for breath is leant on. Inward, away from the rough and warmth of the wall, there is movement on the sand, a scurrying of figures passing between the shade and brightness of the sun, a gathering of the men with capes extended coming towards me. I breathe and feel the blood oozing from my shoulders, watching the men advance, turning my head from one to the other and seeing that they have changed: they are less bright, the fabric they hold faded to a weak and soiled pink – and even the yellow sand they have walked over to enter the shadow, and that I see between the gaps of their encirclement, has lost its straw-like hue.

There is pain at my shoulders, a dull scraping as if a bird has its beak or claws inside the wound and investigates, a sensation almost silenced by the rush of hot blood around it: blood that both carries this pain away into insignificance and sharpens the sight of men in front of me. They stand in clear relief against the sand and the structure behind them, solidifying as the colour leaks from them, becoming firmer objects as if I did not see them clearly before. I push from the wall to stand free of it, the first dropping of a hoof causing a ripple of sound outward, a slight shifting of the men as it touches them.

My head turns to each one of their grouping, quick movements in the indecision of curiosity, the smell of the horse's blood rising as my nostrils clear, its prone and dying form removed from view as I turn away from it, to look across the line of men and wonder at what possibility exists here, now that they are altered, that they or I have changed. There is fear in me, a slipperiness to my breaths and heartbeat, my muscle still humming with its recent movement but my head above it uncertain enough that I lift it to look again to the long and curving wall, for the opening that is hidden: a movement of neck that compresses the wound at my withers and streaks a real and alarming pain down into my legs, a thing sharp and emerging above the roar of blood so that I must drop my head away from it.

But a full step forward and the fear is gone, and instead I am infused with the rush of movement, the first clatter of my hooves driving all doubt into the sound that begins to flow and undulate behind me as I charge, bringing my head up to watch the men as they are drawn closer, a bolt of pain like a solid object that my head bangs against coming from the wound so that I must lower it slightly, away from this beam, but not low enough that I cannot see them, cannot see their stances change and their bodies stiffen as they wait for which one of them I will choose. And the choice itself is lost in the fire in which I lower the points, a grey figure with cape like the others, the heat in my head and neck holding nothing from the sun, coming only from my blood as I charge at the first man and pass him to the next, twisting my legs to turn sharply and gouge, the flap of their capes a snapping at my back, the occasional pressure at the end of a horn a frustrating lightness after the mass of the horse, but enough that I must keep twisting and bursting forward, leading with one horn and then the other as they dance and slide around me, looking again for the impact against them.

It is breath again that stops this frenzy, the lack of it halting me amongst a scattering of men, raising my head until the beginning of pain so that I stand with neck outstretched, my eyes flitting to the bright grey-blue above, nostrils flared at this expanse as if to inhale it entirely. The figures closest to me are brighter and their shadows dark, and as I gasp I feel the sun on my back, to know that I have emerged into the lit crescent of the ring with some of them, the heat from above starting to press gently on me as my own subsides. But with no movement except the laboured heaving of my chest this heat intensifies, growing quickly so that suddenly I am trapped between its crushing weight above and the boiling in my veins, the air between these things warmed to a thinness that does little to fill my lungs. And the figures around me – as I stand and am rocked with breathing I see that one of them struggles too and is limping towards the wall. His disappearance into it becomes the dispersal of the others: they withdraw from their uneven circle around me, walking sideways or backward, one of them without the poised and deliberate walk of the others, disfigured by the clutching of his abdomen – a difference I can only pursue with my eyes, the furnace around me putting a wall of flame before my snout to keep me still.

I look dully through this haze at the appearance of a darker figure, present to the side, not close but approaching over the sand towards me and unobscured by any out-held wing or cape. My neck turns to see this thing fully, the wall behind seeming to undulate above and below it, before I realise that this is the movement of my head, still ruled by lust for the air it pants at. The figure comes closer with slow and deliberate steps and I think that it is like a long-legged bird, made into a man and stalking me as if I were a lizard in grass, a small thing that must be pounced down on. I move my hind legs around to straighten the line between us, my lungs suddenly filling with the sound that this movement triggers: the banks beyond the wall stirring from their murmur, awakened by the fresh intent that is creeping up my neck.

The slow trot forward, the sliding from this into a tight gallop to bring the slender figure closer is a movement I am grateful for, the suffocating heat lifting as soon as the air begins to pass over me, to become something left behind. And with the air running over my back and under my stomach, I realise that I do not rush towards an intrusion, an enemy that must be fought, removed from my surroundings – because there is nothing here, no growth or possibility, nothing now to protect or be fearful for except perhaps the lapsing of my own sensation. The figure I bring towards me is not a threat but simply a part of my desire for immersion, to be held under the liquid of movement and pain and the pain of others that I have inflicted – uncaring for any pause that might return the colour to my eyes. And I wonder that I used my eyes for anything other than this destruction, that I used their focus to bring a small object closer, the same object that withers beneath the sun, or is crushed or blown away. Far better to run like this, seeing only grey shades and an object's distance from my horns, the red liquid around my eyes and over my head and snout not the horses' blood but the colour that has leached from my vision, that renders everything frighteningly clear, a terror that is simply overcome by the dispersal of this clarity: the tossing and gouging of horns into its canvas to make it muddied and soiled, unable to reach out with any sharpness.

This I do now with my lowering of horns to mix and swirl the air before them, watching as the figure becomes more bird-like in the raising of its spindle wings towards me: two white and feathered extensions of its arms drawn up as I close in, as if the beginning of flight – but the man does not take off or leap, he waits until I am nearly on him before stepping to the side, a movement that without the cape to hide it registers clearly even as I swipe upward with a horn to see the skeleton wings descend, a thin but punching impact at my shoulder, a different feel of metal bouncing from the bone there as my head comes up and the horn sweeps across the man's chest. But it does not touch and I slash through nothing but air, able to see the man bend his spine outward to evade me, his arms stretched out and one of the white lengths spinning away as if snapped off. Then he is gone and I am standing, the need for breath immediate and severe, the lack of motion beginning to lever open those parts of me that can be frightened, so that I stand and feel fear ooze from my lungs and stomach, a leaking bile that makes me lift my head and look again to the wall for the opening, a movement as unwilled as recent more violent movements, made emptily and without certainty.

But this doubtful look is blinked away by the discovery of the barb in my withers, a piece of metal that I sense, calmly and without shock, a claw hooked there that my flesh squeezes around when I begin to raise my neck, long tendrils of coolness and pain pulsing from it outward, like the roots of a shading tree that must travel through me to reach the ground. And I am not afraid to have it there, this comfort, because it is a new and vibrant heart that I encourage by crushing it between neck and shoulders, pressing on the kernel of pain this way so that it pumps not blood but spirit into my head, lifting the eyes and horns high to pass through the beam that held them down, into an air where fear is insignificant next to what I can hear and see, the older blood within me rising to escape and flow down one side of my flank, to course up my neck and move my head from side to side, scanning the dull but sharp surrounds in search of fresh hostility.

And when I see the dark figure moving colourlessly towards

me in an identical stalk to the first, his movements are shocking in their clarity, every step to the slightest twitch of his face connected to my eyes, so that in beginning for him I know that he will not evade me. I trot towards him with my head up and wait for his movement, feeling his breaths and blinking ripple against my sight and into my hooves that are suddenly ruled by this vision, their swishing over the dirt controlled and patient as the man's wings open to raise the barbs, a gesture that bolts me forward and plunges my horns down in anticipation of his sideways movement, able to see the distortion I have caused in him before catching the edge of his waist to twist and bend him further – a thin tension I press against to spin him around, the feathered sticks he held loosed into a useless flight.

Suddenly there is a roaring sound to make the air thick and booming as I turn in it, a noise like a pulse of shock and expectation – something to slide against as my legs jar and totter with the tight rotation of the mass above. I revolve to find not a single vulnerable figure, limping after the glancing blow and that I might run down and pound cleanly – but the mass of them: the men with capes, streaming out onto the sand towards me, a sudden cramming of my vision with their floating movement. Amongst them I see the darker figure, the one I caught, another man at his side as if they are joined, heading towards the wall and I think that I will run for this amalgamation when I am startled by the same dark figure suddenly reappearing from behind the loose rope of men that has contracted around me: a black litheness that darts forward with the barbs he holds already extended, an eagerness I match with a quick turn and jolt forward, my head raised and watching all of him down to his feet as we both narrow the ground between us, the sound in the air hanging in a softness until it crashes deafeningly with the stabbing action we make together: the barbs he brings down on me cutting and tearing at my shoulder and neck but not holding; the horns I rake at him catching his leg so that for a brief moment I feel his weight in my neck, a thing I try to scoop with a swinging movement out and upward, but which comes up holding nothing.

I have turned to see the dark figure sprawled on the ground, pulling his limbs beneath him to push upward, a weakling aspect to this struggle that sucks me forward compulsively: he a simple object that must be clattered to feed the thrill and ecstasy of this movement, but which is suddenly obstructed by the out-held fabric of another who has appeared to protect him, so that I must endure again the rustling of the cape over my horns and back. The repetition of impact and feeling – it eludes me, is taken away from me just as I think that it is mine! I run from man to man with nothing from this effort but charging forward at the same enemy suddenly somewhere else, twisting and throwing my head at emptiness, each lack of contact or its result allowing fear to burst like the breaking apart of cold stones inside my body, a panic forming like another liquid in my veins to make the wetness on my back and running down my side a sudden terror.

Then I am stopped and panting, only two men remaining in my vision: the last of their number that have not dissolved against the wall and a pair I am content to share the air with, the need to fill my lungs and stop their agonising gnashing for this substance stronger than any other impulses – which even now as I take long heaving strokes of breath to undulate my spine I can feel massing underneath: fear and lust slipping over and around excitement, a tumult that thunders through my body and that I can feel my heart pound with, the noise of these chambers thumping up my neck to raise my head, the rhythm that throbs in my eyes and ears and in the liquid flowing from my back echoed in the air around me, the low beat of my heart changing to a sharper cracking that swirls around the wall of the ring and the swarming banks above it.

This the sound of me, heading skyward in a column. And when I look down from the sky, away from its ashen brightness to the duller clarity of the sand in the middle of which I am standing, I find that I am alone, the last two men have vanished – that there is nothing here with me except the cadenced cracking of the air. But each breath pulled in without movement allows the entrance of heat, and fear, as if it and fire lie in the air that I must suckle greedily, a poison to seep outward from my lungs and sour all memory of movement, make every recent extension of bone and the flesh wrapped around it useless and unpleasant. I stand with my head upraised, crushing the barb in my shoulders, stretching my neck up against this metal and the torn muscles there so that the pain pulsates out from it madly, a cold blaring that I squeeze and nurture to block my other senses, open as they suddenly are now to the deadly emptiness of the ring, the lack of enemy – the enemy I long for to trigger movement away from the growth of fresh and useless memory, petrifying around my skin.

My heart still fills my head with blood, the horns above it still searing with heat, and I find the sickening tumult within lessening when I sense the change in the sound of the air: the sudden ceasing of its restless clapping, a near silence pervading it. I have learnt that this sound in this space brings forward a new enemy, and with fresh eagerness I turn my head in search of it, looking from the greater area of shaded sand to the smaller crescent of sunlight away from me, a glare stripped completely of its yellow and merely a brightness – and emerging from which is a solitary figure, his head disfigured by the bulbous extensions at its top, his feet visible beneath the smaller wing of fabric that extends below his waist.

He is like the other men, hidden behind their capes, but his walk is different, not only because I can see his feet padding on the sand but because he contains an intent that is like a smell, or the warning cry of a bird – an intent that is directed like his eyes towards me, and in which I search for myself, a sudden desperation to see the image I have become dominant enough to lurch me forward in a stuttering step. The man is at the line of shade and about to step into it, still bright and dazzling until he takes a further step and clarity descends on him like water, his eyes pale and large and emerging from them a shadow: an outline of head and horns that I both recognise and find alien, as if they are mine, but also his.

For a moment silence descends on us, a brief instant when my heart is paused before its next beat and my lungs are at the top of their inflation, a silence that spreads outward from my form and above the sand and the wall around it, stretched to an unknown length by the fixedness of our eyes on the other, the bull I can see thrashing against its human cage within the figure ahead before the myriad murmurings and rustlings begin again with the next beat of my heart, the squeezing of lungs to expel the heated air, the man to take another step towards me. And as he draws nearer, a mixture of caution and aim in the small steps he takes, I find simply that I must destroy him, that I must ruin him and his bearing because he holds more than just the small cape in his hand, he carries in his posture and its formal intent the reality of my alteration, the history of youth and weakness through to the discovery of strength – the sloughing of paddock and all accumulation, all gathering and protection – and the impossibility, once wakened, of ever returning to this sleep.

Yet my lifting of hoof to place it in the trot towards him is hardly mine, is almost distant from my will, a necessary movement to bring me closer to what it is I desire, the lust to have him speared and broken suddenly a separate thing in my mind, separate from the gallop that has formed to patter on the sand – and even as I watch him place his feet and raise the fabric out to me, even as I lower my head and swing it to the side I feel a distance from these actions, a confusion as I emerge with the cape scouring my back into the loud and unified call of many voices, sounds no longer fused to my merest will but a vivid sign of the beast that surrounds me, that I must fight against, that has emerged from the cape itself a separate thing. I turn and the pain in turning, the grinding of the joints in my twisted legs, is suddenly laboured, as if no longer evidence of my own power, the cost of its revolution a poor reflection of the same movement made more perfectly – and rushing for the man again and the savage swinging of head from side to side to try to get at him, this too no longer consumes me fully, a separating from actions only recently gorged on.

Each run and useless lowering of horns, each swinging of them makes no effect but the shared call from the heads surrounding us, a sound I do not create and one that is building to become more detached with every charge, every turn and lengthening pause for breath. And in the moments when I stand and face him, nostrils flared and chest heaving, the lust for impact becomes stronger and more desperate, as if just the edge of one horn to wound him will restore me within the ring, will place me at its centre where all that can be sensed or done is a part of me, is mine. Even in this storm of movement and frustration I am not fully here, I fear the shadow half of me has returned to the barn, and there in the quiet and the darkness it is secretly harbouring memory, making with it things that I want for the man now before me: a mass of perfect destructions that my actions cannot recreate, that spawns only a new frenzy of running and turning to run again, without hesitation, with no thought of breath or the pain in my lungs or at my shoulders until I no longer see the man and the shifting wing he holds but merely an object, a thing that with every thundering pass I begin to suck inward, neither seeing nor hearing it but feeling it as a growth at my flank or the end of my horn – a fragile growth more important than any other, that even in blindness and the rage of my blood I can step over and nurture until it is a part of me, becomes a heavy contact against my flank – the certainty of unwanted impact that pushes him away but not beyond the cast of my awareness, that holds him in my eyes at the end of turning, his posture altered, his own breathing quick and hard, some hair loosened beneath the black protuberance on his head.

His arm rises and the hand at the end of it straightens this covering, a gesture streaked with uncertainty, like the sound that only now begins to make its way to my ears – not the uniform chanting of before but a crackling rumble of doubt, like the fissure of a stone, a stone I crush beneath my weight. I can only stand and gasp, immobile with the overpowering need to satisfy my lungs, a screaming there that is almost the re-binding of the things around me, that makes me feel the stretching of something between us as the man turns and walks towards the wall, his back an invitation, the spark of heat beneath an involuntary half-lifting of a hoof. I watch as the man, standing near the wall, raises his hand, lifting something long and thin above it, a quick twisting of the wrist there to transform its dull wooden edge to that of metal, the glinting briefly glimpsed before it disappears and he has turned and begun walking back to me.

The sound quietens, a fusion of its own prospect and my own, the man coming closer so that I raise my head as if tugged with each deliberate stepping of his approach, until he is only a pace away and my neck is lifted enough to clasp the flesh against the single barb at my shoulders. He extends the grey patch of cape before me, close enough that the air from my nostrils moves it away and my nose can feel the waft of its return. Then the sheet is moving, the man flicking it towards me, triggering weak impulses to charge that are lost somewhere in my mass, that do not have the strength to provoke me forward – because it is not the thing I am watching, not the image in my mind that I await and have seen before: the rising of the arms in the arcing lunge to barb my shoulders. This is what I hope for, and I lower my head to entice it from him, knowing it is a movement I can catch, a thing both beyond me but which I have made, the tendrils from my senses reaching out to his form as he stands there, flapping the cape at me, a new growth of excitement sprouting towards him and upward from my spine.

Shrill cries and whistles begin to emerge from the deepened quiet, distant and angered sounds that are not born of my patience as I wait. I wonder if they might come from the man – who on hearing them makes the slightest of movements, the lightest shifting of weight from one leg to the other, the prelude I know before the hips turn and the back is exposed, a movement I have seen before and recognise as clearly as the opening of a gate, just such a movement shown to me with similar taunting, in the ring of the farm, that ended with a lifeless slumping shape. The man has not even begun to turn when he sees me lunge forward, is balanced enough that he can take a step back as I raise my head before lowering it, my eyes level with the top of the fabric he holds, able to see the blade that emerges as he whips the cape to the side before my vision is dragged down by the punching forward of the horns, the sand close and very distinct, a landscape of undulation and ripple. Then there is darkness as I raise my head – an absolute darkness as I strain forward with the horns, stretching everything of neck and leg to reach further, my eyes closed to better feel it, to better anticipate the weight that does not come, that does not burden my neck as I lift my head and open my eyes, a new pain in my withers, sharp and pure, deeper than the barb.

I stand and raise my head, pointing the horns upward, feeling the cool metal in my back, the blood beginning to trickle again over the blood hardened earlier, to escape down from my shoulders and run against the back of my foreleg. The fresh and un-barbed point scratches at the bone above my heart and lungs, but no deeper – yet it has severed something, this attack, it has cut the sound away from me and any movement I might make: a baying and crying that pours from the banks of men and women to fill the ring, waves of sound that yearn for something I do not recognise, that may be inside me also but I would rather trample on: this thick sound and cloying plea rising slowly until it feels as if it is up to my chin, that I might choke in it, mired dumbly in its mud to watch the man disappear against the curved wood around the ring, expecting him or others like him to return – but they do not – and I am left alone to splash through the unchanging sound, taking a few steps in unwilled directions, a difficult and uncertain pacing, made in a rising clamour of pain and tiredness.

And then a darkness appears in the wall: a true aperture unblocked by any figure, any distraction of cape or armoured horse, so that I do not avert my head and can see it perfectly clearly: a sharp-sided opening leading to more darkness beyond, to a stall perhaps and the shell it makes and I turn to this, the weight of my flesh suddenly crushing in my legs, to make me fear that I cannot move them. But it is the sound and its will that washes me towards it, as if I do not need to lift my hooves, as if I am trapped in something giant and draining, a flow I cannot fight against, I do not wish to fight against, the bank and its multitude of eyes above the entrance looming as I near it, the cap of sky diminishing as with quickened steps I leave the ring, the blood still in my head and coursing strongly as I pierce the darkness, my heart unharmed to push it there, the blade that sought it worked free by the blades of my shoulders to fall away, to become a futile clattering on the ground.

quickened steps I leave the ring, the blood still in my head and coursing strongly as I pierce the darkness, my heart unharmed to push it there, the blade that sought it worked free by the blades of my shoulders to fall away, to become a futile clattering on the ground.